The Horror Collection
White Edition

Presented by
Kevin J. Kennedy

The Horror Collection: White Edition © 2019
Kevin J. Kennedy

Edited by Becky Narron

Cover design by Michael Bray

First Printing, 2019

Other Books by KJK Publishing

Anthologies

Collected Christmas Horror Shorts

Collected Easter Horror Shorts

Collected Halloween Horror Shorts

Collected Christmas Horror Shorts 2

The Horror Collection: Gold Edition

The Horror Collection: Black Edition

The Horror Collection: Purple Edition

100 Word Horrors

100 Word Horrors: Part 2

100 Word Horrors: Part 3

Carnival of Horror

Novels and Novellas

Pandemonium by J.C. Michael

You Only Get One Shot by Kevin J. Kennedy & J.C. Michael

Screechers by Kevin J. Kennedy & Christina Bergling

Collections

Dark Thoughts by Kevin J. Kennedy

Vampiro and Other Strange Tales of the Macabre
by Kevin J. Kennedy

Foreword

This is the fourth book in The Horror Collection series. This series was set up to allow me to do some mini-anthologies which were easier to squeeze in between other projects. The Collected Horror Shorts books are much longer, and I struggle to find the time to put them together these days. The Horror Collection books are normally about 20K but this one is almost double the length.

I decided to do a Christmas version as part of the collection and got to work with some authors I had never worked with before as well as some regular KJK Publishing names you will know.

Christmas is one of my favourite times of year and I always used to find that there wasn't a great deal of Christmas-themed horror out there. This was the reason I put my first-ever anthology together... to try and fix a hole in the market. Since then there have been a load of Christmas-themed horror anthologies released, but I think we can all handle one more.

The stories in this book were my favourites of the ones that were submitted, and I think you will have a lot of fun with them.

I'd like to wish you a Merry Christmas, wherever you are and whatever you are doing, from everyone at KJK Publishing. I hope this book helped put a smile on your face.

Table of Contents

'Twas the Night Before Yuletide
By
James Matthew Byers

'Twas the night before Yuletide,

And all through the land
Santa Claus was preparing

To make Christmas grand.
He went out to his stables,

His heart full of cheer,
In a last ditch planned effort

To rouse his reindeer.

The snow falling brutally

As each crisp step cracked
And Saint Nicholas carried

The toys he had packed.
When he entered the stables,

Two ravens sat perched.
All around them were symbols;

The wood grains red smirched.

"Now, pray, what is the matter?

What mean you birds here?
Have you come to cause trouble

Among my reindeer?"
The two ravens said nothing,

Then flew to the door.
Upon flitting, then quitting,

They said, "Nevermore."

"Nevermore?" Santa quoted,

"Pray, what does that mean?
In a thousand past years,

This beats all I have seen!"
Then they gave a good chuckle

With wicked delight.
"Nevermore will you travel

On Christmas Eve night!"

A look of surprise as

The caws burst in cackle,

And Santa Claus saw Dasher

Break from his shackle.
Then the ravens flew out

As the reindeer stood tall,
Captivating Saint Nick,

Who in fear took a fall.

"By the power of Christmas,

What meaning is this?
Tell me, Dasher, now tell me!

Just what is amiss?"
"Weihnachtsmann, some people,

They know me as Woden.
In Asgard, I rule.

I am Allfather, Odin!

Much too long have you punished

These wood folk I see ...
As the Lord of the Hunt,

I will now set them free."
And as Odin spoke, magic

Dispersed from each beast.
"They are reindeer no longer;

Each soul is released."

Santa stood in much anger,

Scoffed, "We will just see.
Odin, you with your antlers

Can't take them from me!
Now just look at you, fool,

As some reindeer like god-
I will give you a whacking

With my lashing rod!"

And as Santa approached

Swinging hard left and right,
Out of nowhere, the ravens

Dropped something in sight.
Odin reached and snatched Gungnir,

His magical spear,

Hoof like hands holding on

As a battle drew near.

Father Christmas smashed hard

With the rod in his hand,
But the spear Odin blocked with

Had much more command.
Back and forth the two parried,

With nary a break,
And then Odin transformed

Christmas lights to a snake.

After glow in its making,

The brightly lit thing
Made its way around Santa,

Who started to sing
All the names of the reindeer,

But he was ignored.
The serpent squeezed tighter,

Santa cried, "I adored

Each and all of the reindeer

That pulled on my sleigh.
And now look at you creatures!

My, how you betray!"
From the shadows, the eighth one

That Odin had been
Came and offered to Santa,

"The age of these men

Now is ending for we are

The dwellers who seek
To repay all the wicked

And prey on the weak.
No more presents and falsehoods

From you in your lie.
Know that Midgard is free,

As are we, so now die!"

Saint Nick slumped to his side

And died in the stable,
The folk of the woodlands

Placed him on a table.
And as Odin then gathered

His things and took flight,
"Merry Yule," they exclaimed

As they all took a bite...

Christmas Eve
By
Mark Tufo

"Christmas Eve. I'm out in this shit show on Christmas eve!" Devan Andrews shouted over the steering wheel of his sizable brown delivery truck. He was looking out at the heavy snow that fell, it turned a garish blend of reds and greens through the lens of Christmas lights as they crystallized upon the windshield, his wipers doing little to keep the precipitation from building up. The city had already declared an emergency, warning people to stay off the streets, but that hadn't prevented his boss from sending him out to deliver last-minute gifts for those too lazy to have done it sooner. Anger welled up in him as he double-parked on the busy main street, but a satisfied smile splayed across his face as he heard the irritated horns of several motorists attempting to get around.

"The governor said to stay home. You should have," he said as he stood from his seat and opened up the partition doorway to gain access to the cargo hold. Devan hadn't always been an angry young man, in fact, far from it. He had grown up in a loving home, spent a carefree childhood in the rolling hills of Maryland. The Andrews' had not been rich, but he'd never wanted for anything. He'd had many friends, been popular in high school, lettered in three separate sports. His future, while not the burning brightness of stardom, still shone a steady illumination that would have allowed him to walk far within its light. He'd received four scholarships, he could have gone anywhere. Instead, he'd settled for his home state, wanting to stay close to all that he knew. In his Junior year, he met the most perfect woman; she would perfectly be his undoing.

Darcy Deneaux was a tall blonde drink of water, one he was sure he would never quench his thirst for. At the conclusion to his senior year, her junior year, she'd approached him with the news that she was pregnant. Not wanting to upset her parents, who were devout Christians, he had asked her to marry him on the spot, and a month later, they were standing in front of a Justice of the Peace. Devan didn't think his life could be any more perfect.

The months began to pass, but Darcy did not "show," nor did she make any doctor's appointments. He was at first concerned, then suspicious, but every time he asked her about it, she flew off the handle and started a fight that would quickly devolve into great bouts of crying; on more than one occasion she physically assaulted him. It got to the point where he could not even bear the thought of broaching the subject.

Darcy's discontent did not stop there. She continually abused Devan verbally, to the point that he was no longer able to perform in the bedroom, which brought further ridicule and disgust. He was ashamed and becoming more isolated by the day. Darcy would rail on him, boasting that she was going out to find a "real man" to take care of her needs. She would come back hours later, sometimes the next morning, and tell him in detail all that she'd done. He would sit on the couch, crying, as she did this. For five years he lived in this hell until the day when he came home from work, and their apartment had been cleaned out—except for the couch—which she had taped a note to. She'd left him for a lawyer in Virginia. He'd not contested any of their possessions; they'd lost their value to him, much like the marriage. All he had were the clothes he was wearing and the baby's education fund he had been planning on surprising her with and then wisely hidden from her.

He'd not told anyone where he was going the day he went to the bus depot and bought a one-way ticket to New York City. He figured he could get lost in the sea of humanity; no one would know him, and none would ask about his past. He found a motel barely above a flea-bag rating and set about looking for work. It was UPS that hired him the following week; loading and unloading packages became his life. After four years, he was promoted to delivery driver, a position he coveted, mistakenly believing he would no longer need to talk to anyone, not even his coworkers. How wrong he'd been about that. Most of the customers on his route were regulars who seemed to have nothing better to do than to share their life stories. He smiled and nodded at all the appropriate times, but inside he was screaming at them to shut their stupid fucking mouths.

That Christmas Eve night, he punched two boxes out of the way, happy when he heard the telltale tinkle of something breaking. "Aw, little Johnnie is going to be so upset that his Thanos doll's got no jewels." A gust of freezing wind and a blast of snow greeted him as he headed around the back and rolled up the freight door. He zipped up his jacket and stacked up his dolly. He'd no sooner got the dolly rolling when an errant breeze grabbed hold of the topmost padded envelope and sent it spiraling into the street. Devan spun and bent to grasp the package before it could blow away and be lost forever. He was shocked by the blistering sound of a held down horn and the brightness of headlights approaching him at a speed much greater than prudent, given the elements. "Fuck you!" he shouted. As he spun and stood back up, vertigo threatened to put him on his ass. He tried to shake off the sudden bout of lightheadedness as the city lights dimmed around him and the sound fell away. Devan was afraid he was going to pass out, and then as suddenly as it had come on, it was over.

"That was weird. Probably just dehydrated." He was thinking on the fifth of gin he had killed last night, something he wished he were repeating this very moment. He walked into the office building, the anger, which had abated, now came roaring back as he realized there were no security guards at the front desk. Without them, he could not gain access to the elevators. "You have got to be shitting me. Now I'm going to get a shitload of complaints." He yelled out for anyone; his echo came back empty. He had just turned his dolly to head out when he heard the dinging of an elevator opening. "My lucky day!" he snarked as he ran back. He just got the toe of his boot in between the closing doors, and they popped back open. He was going to sarcastically thank whoever was in there for "holding the door," when he realized he was alone.

"Whatever," he said as he checked the floor number of the top package. "Seventy-seven? Good a place to start as any. What the hell kind of name is Elan Duel? Sounds French. I wonder if I'll get tipped with a bagel."

When the elevator door opened at his desired floor, he'd almost been too surprised to step out. He was in the foyer of what could only be described as Gothic mansion. Two broad, curving staircases were on either side. Tall, thick candles sat atop bronze holders, the accumulated wax of their brethren coating the sides in thick, grey tallow. As he stepped out, he looked up to see a crystal chandelier some thirty feet above; fifty candles burned brightly and cast dancing shadows on the far walls. Past that, a ten-foot tall statue of a winged female looked down upon him. Her expression was distinctly sad, as if what she'd seen happening below had tortured her soul.

"Must know my wife," Devan quipped. The walls up the staircases were decorated with antique silvered mirrors and portraits done in age-darkened oils. All the subjects wore similar forlorn expressions. "Looks like a fun place to work." The only place he saw to drop the package off (and get out of this strange place) was straight ahead, across the room, through an arched entryway. As he stepped across the threshold, his vision was blinded momentarily by a dazzling white light; he thought perhaps it was due to the nature of the room he now found himself in. In direct contrast to the lavish architecture he'd just left, this room was stark; a postmodern minimalism. There was nothing in the entirety of it save one desk placed squarely in the middle. It made about as much sense as the rest of the place. The rent on this space, he knew, was more than he made in three years. It should have been wall-to-wall with offices and cubes, fitting as many workers inside as was allowable by law.

A substantial leather chair turned, and the sole occupant of floor seventy-seven turned to greet the driver.

"Devan, Devan. Welcome!" the man said.

Devan found himself rooted to the spot; there was something about that too-big smile and the affable way the man called out. That was not something that happened in New York, not ever. People kept their heads down and eye contact to a minimum.

"Mr. Duel, you've got a package. Just need you to sign here." Devan held out the bulky signature pad.

"Of course, of course," Elan said as he stood. He wrapped an arm around Devan's shoulder and escorted him in. The man was a head taller than Devan, who himself stood just over six-feet. He had seemed much smaller, seated in the broad leather chair, and as he approached, it was as if every step taken had gained him height. By the time they got back to the desk, Devan was certain the man had gained another foot in stature. "Sit, sit, take a load off."

"I, umm, really should be going." Devan was looking around for something, anything as he sat uncomfortably. "It being Christmas Eve and all, I've got to finish my deliveries and get back home."

"To the kiddos?" Elan asked. Though his smile registered as friendly, his eyes were predatory. The tone indicated he already knew the answer to the question posed.

"Uh, no kids just...you know, got to finish up."

"Don't worry about a thing, Devan. Not your deliveries, nor that bottle of gin you have cooling in the freezer."

Devan shot up. "Now wait a minute. I thought it was weird you knew my name but...but..." he stammered.

"A guess! A lucky guess, I assure you. Now sit." It was not a request.

"What is this place?"

"May I have my package?"

Devan handed it over. Elan ripped the tab open and extracted an ornate pen with gold inlays and a tip that required it be dipped into a bottle of ink, which Devan now noticed sat upon the desk.

"That wasn't there a second ago."

"Of course it was; it's always been there."

"I've got to go," Devan said, though he did not stand.

"But we have not concluded our appointment."

"Appointment?"

"I have you down for precisely seven sixteen, December twenty-fourth."

"Mister—I've never met you, and I certainly didn't make an appointment with you."

"Most don't bother, but it's of no matter." He smiled, flashing larger than life teeth.

"I don't understand what's going on here." Devan gripped the arms of his chair tightly, fighting back an urge to shake which once started, he feared he would not be able to stop.

"It's Christmas Eve Devan; I'm offering a

present the like of which only happens once in a lifetime and only to a handful of worthy people."

"Oh, I get it...is this like Undercover Boss?" Devan eased some and looked around for the hidden cameras.

"Not quite. There was a person in your life, a woman. She didn't treat you right. In fact, she took more away from you than just your new Mustang and your 4k television. Am I right?" Elan asked. Devan turned to the side and crossed his legs self-consciously as he noticed that Elan was unabashedly staring at his lap. Elan laughed and held out his pinkie finger, repeatedly curling it over.

Devan stood then. "What the fuck kind of show is this?" He was angrier than he could ever remember being and he balled up his fists. He thought the rage might have a lot to do with the underlying fear coursing through him like a current of low voltage.

"Sit...sit! Just a little jest; although perhaps it was in poor taste."

"Perhaps?" Devan had not yet sat down.

"What if I told you there was a way to get back at her."

"I am not a vengeful person."

"There are no cameras; what you say here is between you and me," Elan responded.

"Like I said."

"You would wish the woman who cut short your potential, emasculated you, took all your worldly possessions, and described in vivid detail all her—let's say indiscretions—to you...you would wish this woman well?"

"That never came out of my mouth."

"You don't wish her well; you don't wish her ill. That is the story of your life, is it not?"

"What are you talking about?"

"We will get to the good stuff soon enough, I suppose." Elan lifted a sheet of paper from the desktop that Devan had not seen previously and placed it into a drawer. "I'll state this simply in ways a mortal can understand."

"What does that mean?"

Elan held up his hand. "In due time. There is a war being waged between good and evil, you know this; all humans know this. In all likelihood, it will never be resolved. It is a war waged for the sake of war, really." Elan pondered his words for a moment before shaking his head and resuming. "Each side is granted soldiers; for ease of reference we'll say ten percent of the population each. These are your true saints and sinners, your Mother Teresas and your Hitlers, your Mahatma Gandhis and your Jeffrey Dahmers. These, and millions of others, fought exclusively for their respective sides, naturally disposed. But the majority of people, we'll say seventy percent, are placed on a team because of their actions during life, rescue babies from burning buildings, garner good points. Slit the throats of strangers and watch the blood pour out, well, bad points, I suppose." Elan smiled at that. "You get the idea, right?"

Devan nodded, though he couldn't see the point to any of this.

"The remaining percentage, somewhere around ten, they're like you. The neutrals. They walk through life so mundanely as to not garner attention from either side. Never understood that about your lot. You are given one go around, and yet you make not the slightest ripple in the pool of existence. That's more pathetic than the fools who devote their entire lives to helping the downtrodden. I mean, live a little! Am I right?" Elan's voice boomed throughout the room, a glint of fire flashed through his eyes.

"I...I don't understand," Devan beseeched.

"You're a dullard, my boy. What's not to understand? No good, no bad. You just are, like a pebble in the desert."

"Are you the devil?"

"The devil? What an antiquated notion. A human appellation if ever there was one."

Devan failed to notice if the other answered the question.

"Perhaps we should get back to the

business at hand." The sheet of paper was back upon the desktop, though Devan had not seen him move to put it there. "Your ex-wife, that deliciously wicked creature. You wish to repay her for her, let's say, transgressions?"

"Look, mister...I just want to get out of here. You've got your package. If you could just sign...you know what...forget it. I'll sign off on it, no one will know the difference."

"Look at you, Devan! Already taking a step to the wild side. How's it feel? Are you finally able to..." He glanced at the other man's crotch again and quickly moved his eyebrows up and down.

"Can we not talk about that anymore?" Devan was turned and made a few steps toward the archway, until he realized it was no longer there. "It...it was right there. I need to get out of here."

"Once our business is concluded, of course."

"What business?"

"Dull and stupid is not a good combination for anyone, Devan. We've established that you are of the mundane ten percenters. Good so far? Or do you need an interpreter? You know, someone to dumb   it   down. Would...it...help...if...I...spoke...slower?"

"I understand."

"Good. Now sit the fuck down, as I asked!" Again, Elan's voice boomed, the resultant echo somehow louder than the original source.

Devan felt compelled to do as he was told.

"Now, this is where it gets interesting. Your God, whoever that may be…"

"I'm an atheist."

"Oh, splendid. How did I not know that tidbit? Matters little. Your 'Not God' would have dismissed you out of hand. She has little patience for those who pay her no mind. You'd be relegated to the eternal grayness of purgatory; that place is like eating unsweetened oatmeal for every meal for the rest of all eternity. But I'm here to save you from all of that." Elan shuddered; a plume of smoke involuntarily escaped his mouth. "Sorry. I had live baby lamb smothered in Carolina Reaper pepper sauce. I thought I knew what hot was! I'm worried about later tonight…know what I mean?" He laughed as he lifted his ass off his seat.

"I'm not sure what any of this has to do with me."

"I'm giving you a chance to escape that eternal blah."

"If any of what you 're saying is true, which I doubt, by the way, as soon as I leave here, I'm going to sign up to work at a soup kitchen and earn some good points."

"Little late for that."

"I have plenty of time."

"Even those in their eighties say that same thing when they're here. When they're right there. I'm glad you're sitting, because this part usually comes as a big shock. Being that I'm immortal, I can't even imagine what your lot goes through, but I do love the myriad responses I get. Anger, sadness, denial…most of all desperation. Whoo…ready for the big reveal?" he asked, furiously rubbing his hands together. "Too much? I'm told it makes me look like a 1920s movie villain."

"I'm going to be late for the rest of my deliveries."

"Funny you should say 'late.' You really haven't put this together yet? That's a hell of a mental block you have going there. Okay, let me make it easier for you." Elan waved his hand and the entire back wall illuminated into a viewing screen.

"Hey, that's me!" Devan said as he watched himself gather packages in the back of the truck. "I knew they had cameras back there!"

"The denseness is thick in this one," Elan said to no one in particular.

Devan watched and wondered how much trouble he was going to get in for his rough treatment of the packages in his care.

"This is where it gets interesting," Elan remarked as the door in the truck opened to a blustery New York storm.

"Wait...what is happening?" Devan asked as the envelope was lifted into the air and into traffic. "How could the camera angle change?"

"Fair warning: you might want to look away. Gets a little gruesome here." Elan moved closer to get a better look; an expectant smile played out across his face.

Devan gasped as he watched himself lean over. The front end of a Yellow Cab clipped the top of his head and sent a spray of bone, blood and hair into the air. His body was whipped around and collided into the side of the heavy-duty vehicle, impacting it hard enough to dent the door, along with the quarter panel.

"That...that's not what happened! I grabbed the package! I'm here!" He frantically tapped himself to feel the solidity of his existence.

"You're here; that's true enough."

Devan's eyes were riveted to the scene; the screeching halt of tires, the horrified cab driver looking down on what was most assuredly a dead body—the entirety of his skull had been crushed. Distant sirens could be heard as snowflakes fell upon the open and shocked eyes of the shell that had once housed Devan Andrews.

"Seen enough?" Elan asked, shutting off the screen before the other could answer.

"I'm dead?" Devan swallowed hard. "But why? What did I do?"

"It's not a matter of what you did. When it's your time, that's it."

"But you engineered this whole thing. If not for that stupid fucking pen you're holding, I'd still be alive!"

"I'll admit I had some hand in how you died; that's a wish granted to me from time to time, but the when? No, I can't do anything about that. The entity you call Death...his ledgers cannot be altered. Well, that's not entirely true; once in a blue moon someone will...cheat Death, but you have a better chance of winning the lottery while getting struck by lightning. That matters not. What matters is this right here."

"What is 'this right here?'"

"An opportunity, my boy. You're dead; can't argue that fact. I can't give you back what is not mine to give. Just thought I'd throw that out there; this is where a lot of people begin to plead for it. It gets exhausting. Usually they become angry with me for not yielding to their supplication. I've even had people ask to see my manager, as if we were at a fast food restaurant and they want a free order of chicken nuggets for the trouble I've put them through. The nerve of some people," he said good-naturedly.

Devan didn't know whether to laugh or cry. "What do you want from me?"

"It's more like: what do you want from me? Let's get down to business." Elan walked back to his desk and sat down. He leaned across and grabbed Devan's hand. The touch was warm on his rapidly cooling skin. "We don't have much time. You have two choices. We sit around here for a few more minutes until you are called away to the great grayness that is purgatory, where you will wander alone, surrounded by millions like you, forever. Seeing, but never interacting, with those lost souls around you. A punishment far greater than one is deserving, if you ask me. Your benevolent God is anything but to those she does not deem worthy."

"Or?" Devan asked nervously. He'd liked New York for the anonymity, but an eternity?

"There you go thinking ahead. Your ex-wife, one that will be in my realm soon enough..." he mused. "You sign this contract and I will release the one you call Karma on her."

"Karma is an individual, not a thing?"

"Oh, it is most certainly a being, one that, in Darcy's case, has been kept at bay to a standing contract signed many long years ago. Those Deneauxs have an evil that delves deep within them. This, in part, is why Darcy is the way she is. She has never been made to answer for any of the horrid things she has done. If one needn't suffer consequences for their actions, what is to prevent them from doing whatever they please, hmm?" he asked.

"And if I were to sign this?" Devan noticed

that the pen was now in his hand and the contract directly in front of him.

"Well, then the fun begins. I will leave you here and you will watch the entirety of her life unfold, and I would imagine, unravel. Just think; you could exact your revenge, regain your masculinity, revel in the delight of her destruction."

"That's it? I sign this, she gets fucked? And then what?"

Elan let his head gently tap against his desk before looking up and sighing. "What do you think happens? You will have finally committed an act worthy of allowing you to gain entry into a realm."

"I hate Darcy." Devan gripped the pen harder and let the tip rest against the paper.

"Yes." Elan made a steeple with his fingers.

"I loved her once, and she was cruel." Devan pressed harder; a blot of ink formed on the page. "And she deserves this."

"Oh, she most assuredly does."

"But I can't."

"What?!" Elan stood. His eyes changed from a coal black to a fiery red.

"You yourself said she is an evil being. If that's the case, she'll pay for that when she gets here."

"But the revenge will not be yours! Don't be stupid. You could enjoy watching fifty years of a slow-burning torture."

Devan stood. "I live in New York. I haven't said more than twenty words to anyone in the last year, and even that was a bit much. Most of it revolved around not receiving enough change. No, perhaps I'll find the peace I was looking for in purgatory."

"Fool!" Elan began to fade away, the room elongated, the intensity of the white light brightened.

"Merry Christmas!" an angelic voice sang.

"This purgatory?" Devan asked.

"Not exactly." There was an upward lilt to her words, as if she were laughing. "By refusing a great evil, you did a greater good. I think you know where you are."

"Weird, weird day," he muttered. He could not stop smiling as he looked over a great green valley strewn with abundant wildflowers and not another soul in sight.

The End

The Advent of Father Hirst
By
Lex H Jones

From the diary of Father Leopold Dunley

Priest of the Parish of St Luke.

Wednesday 29th November

I arrived at my new church to find it was about half the size of my last one! Which, I must add, brought me to a state of joy, rather than disappointment. I've spent the past four years working out of a city parish, which of course necessitated a much larger church. Not that the size of the congregation these days filled it even to half capacity, but still, a building of that scale can seem intimidating and often did. After the financial scandal, in which the seniors of the church disagreed with my using church funds to help a struggling family, I was forced to move to a more 'out of the way' locale to keep things brushed under the prayer rug. So here I am.

Umberton is a rural village that's on the cusp of becoming a town. I don't know the exact statistics for such a transition, but the mines have brought much business here. On the edge of the town lies a large row of houses that are a newer build than the traditional stone ones, which includes my own clergy house. I daresay they have better heating, plumbing and clearer signals for the television as well. Still I am very happy to be in an area such as this, particularly with Christmas on the approach.

The coming of the festive season really does make my job easier with regard to ingratiating myself into village life. Faith is dying out here, as it is in all places really, so to arrive in the midst of summer with a goal of reigniting it, might seem a little lofty and ambitious. To do so in the Christmas period, however, when even the staunchest disbeliever feels a touch of the spirit in the air, is somewhat easier a task. For one thing, the church is likely to be more full than it would usually, which allows me the opportunity to meet greater numbers of the locals without doing something so intrusive as to knock on each of their doors.

Saturday 2nd December

It's been a strange few days, and that's left me little time to write here. My head's been buried in a diary, but rather curiously not my own. I should elaborate.

It started when I was at the local shop buying a newspaper. An elderly woman introduced herself as Gladys, and asked whether or not I would be lighting the advent this weekend. Now I will admit I shouldn't have been as surprised by this request as I was. Traditions like that had somewhat faded in my previous parish, but it's probably fair to say that they hold on stronger in rural communities. I admitted to Gladys that I hadn't given it any thought, but that if it was a village tradition to do so, then of course I would make an event of it. She then said the most curious thing, which was that it was important I light the advent whether or not it was made a social church event. She also insisted that I kept the advent lit at all times. One candle for each weekend on the approach to Christmas, as is traditional, but still once the first was lit it must remain so constantly, and then once two were lit they must remain so, and so on. I asked her why and she replied simply that it was an important tradition begun by Father Hirst, my predecessor.

I didn't know what to make of this, but gave her my assurance that I would light the advent crown beginning this coming Sunday, and leave it lit. Of course, in reality, keeping it lit at all hours in a drafty village church is somewhat unrealistic. However I will make sure it's lit during the hours when anyone is likely to visit, at the least. That should keep Gladys, and any other parishioners, happy that I am doing my best to maintain village traditions.

Once I arrived back home, I sat down to read the newspaper I'd purchased. The front pages were full of whatever antics that Liverpudlian music group were up to, so I skipped ahead a few pages. It's not that I have no interest at all in whatever movements form part of the current zeitgeist, it's just that I don't feel such things really qualify as news, and they're certainly not why I purchase a newspaper. Still, it seems my attention was not to be fixed for long on current events, regardless of their level of importance.

As I read about the upcoming vote to abolish the death penalty in this country --about time, I must say -- the house grew noticeably colder. Perhaps it was the subject matter, and the voiced opinions in the article that all criminals should be hanged without hesitation, that brought a chill to the air? I can't rightly say, but I noticed that I could now see my breath. The heating in the house was of a rather old-fashioned setup, so my immediate thought was that this was probably to blame.

The boiler was in the corner of the loft, which was accessible by a hatch with a foldout ladder behind it. Sure enough, having made my way into the dusty old loft and come face to face with the boiler, I saw that the pilot light had blown out. As I re-ignited it, I heard a heavy thud behind me. I turned, startled. Nothing else resides in the house besides me -- I have no cat, although I do intend to get one -- so to hear a noise that was beyond the creaking of a floorboard or banging of a pipe, was far from expected.

As I turned, I saw that a wooden chest had fallen from a shelf in the corner of the loft, and now lay facedown on the floor. The shelf on which the chest had resided showed no sign of being loose, so I can only assume that the chest had not been properly balanced, and my sudden presence in the attic had somehow been the catalyst of its sudden disturbance. As for the chest itself, it was around the size of a large hatbox. My curiosity was peaked, so my thoughts immediately turned to opening it. How grateful was I, then, to see that the latch keeping the chest closed was bereft of a lock. Flicking it up was enough to allow the chest to be opened.

Inside the chest was an old church advent crown made of iron, and a thick leather-bound journal. I say 'journal' perhaps a bit hastily, as I didn't immediately recognise it as such and only confirmed this upon opening it. At first glance, I took the journal to be a Bible, given the thickness and weight of it. Indeed there were some passages from the Good Book pasted into it -- photocopied pages, I might add, before you worry that somebody had torn out said pages -- but the majority of the book was the writings of its author, Father Michael Hirst, my predecessor at this parish and the previous occupant of my new home. The journal contained much of his own thoughts, as this diary contains my own, but also a section that was devoted to something of an instruction manual relating to the advent crown.

The instructions detailed how the crown needed to be lit from the first weekend in December, with the second candle being lit from the second weekend, and so on. Fairly standard procedure for a church tradition, I thought. But the instructions then went on to echo what Gladys had said to me; from the first weekend of Advent until Christmas day itself, *'the crown must be kept lit at all times'*. To accomplish this, the candles were in fact hollow, with their faux wicks drawing up from a well of liquid paraffin that filled the hollow middle of the crown. If it were filled daily, this fuel would mean the candles kept burning for almost the entire month of December.

So, despite my previous misgivings, it seemed that keeping the crown constantly lit would not be such a hassle after all. What I still failed to understand was why it was necessary? Traditions are fine and certainly have their place, and I'm hardly the person to deride such things given the nature of my chosen life! But something in the way Father Hirst wrote about it sits ill at ease with me. I can't quite describe it. His instructions aren't simply a matter of *'this is how to use the special Advent Crown'*, but rather an insistence that what he has described *must* be done. Perhaps the rest of his journal provides more details about why he felt this way, but I've not yet had time to peruse it.

I put the journal and the Advent Crown back in the chest, and decided I would bring them downstairs with me. I wasn't yet decided whether or not I'd actually honour the tradition in full, but I'd certainly set the crown in the church. As I closed the chest and lifted it, I caught sight of a shape in the corner of my eye. There, in the far shadows of the loft, a figure stood watching me. I froze. Nobody could have climbed the ladder in the time I'd been up there. Which left the possibility that this person had already been residing in the loft when I ascended the ladder. The notion of a third possibility, which falls more firmly under the realms of the absurd, did occur to me. I shan't say that it didn't.

I did not wish to turn and see whoever might be stood behind me, but I knew that I had little option. So, gathering more courage than logic would suggest is necessary for such a basic act, I turned and demanded the figure told me what they wanted. Sure enough, there was nobody there. Now your thoughts about this are probably that the shape I mistook for a figure was nothing more than the shadows formed by the slanted roof, a coat hung on the wall, a hat-stand perhaps. None of these were the case. There was nothing on that side of the loft that could have formed such a shape in my vision. As I stared into the shadows, I became aware of somebody stood very closely to my left side. I felt their breath upon my face, and I shut my eyes. Whatever this was, I had no wish to see it. A voice whispered in my ear *'light it'* and then the voice, and the source of it, were gone. If, in fact, they had ever been there.

Taking the chest, I left the loft far more hastily than I had climbed up into it. Once in the daylight-filled rooms of the house below, the experience I'd just suffered through seemed the stuff of folly and imagined nonsense. Too much dust, too much shadow, too many nerves set on edge by Father Hirst's feverish writings. It's easy to mock oneself when looking back on these moments, but at the time of their happening they seem terrifyingly real. I am not altogether ashamed to admit that I left the hallway light on as I retired to my bed for the night.

#

Sunday 3rd December

I lit the first of the candles adorning the advent crown this morning. There were about a dozen or so people in the church for the ceremony, most of whom had been present for the Sunday service beforehand but others came late. It'd be easy to take umbrage to that, but I shan't. The village needs to get to know me, and if the way to attract people to the church for now is through the rituals and excitements of the festive period, then I'm perfectly happy with that. I got to meet some new faces and say my hellos, so I think all went rather well.

The lighting of the candle itself went without incident as well. I hadn't had the time to practice beforehand, so the act of filling the crown with paraffin oil -- and not spilling it all over the floor -- had to be conducted for the first time in front of an audience. Thankfully my hands didn't shake, and the stand on which the crown was placed was sturdy. I said the prayers and lead the hymns as given in Father Hirst's instructions, the congregation joining in. The final prayer, however, was said by me alone, owing to the fact that it was in Latin. I will confess that I didn't fully understand it, but it was something about the Light holding back the Darkness that was here before. If truth be told, I rather suspect that Father Hirst wrote that one himself, which put upon me the desire to read more of his journals.

After saying goodbye to the congregation and agreeing to enough invites for tea and Christmas cake to see me through the winter, I was left alone in the church. The candle still burned, and the glass slit in the side of the crown allowed me to see the paraffin levels as though I were checking the fuel level on some crucial machine. I estimated that I'd need to refill it every couple of days, but this would increase in frequency with the lighting of more candles. I can't say that I'm overly concerned about the possibility of the candles going out for a short period, but my experience in the loft yesterday, even if it was assumed to be the product of my imagination, makes me feel as though I ought to be. As I was left alone with these thoughts in the church, I felt a sudden draft blow against my face. Actually no, that's not the correct way to describe it. The draft felt like more of a pull than a push. As though a sudden rush of cold air was being drawn behind me, like a large inhalation.

I turned, and immediately facing me was nothing but the church altar. The altar was made of solid oak, and covered by a red tarp with gold trim. Atop this stood a golden cross and two slim white candles -- a stark contrast to the red ones adorning the advent crown. There was nothing unusual around the altar, but there was the sound of howling wind coming from it, like a crack in the wall of a wind-swept castle. I approached it, and whilst I could no longer feel the pulling draft, the sound got louder as I got closer. I reached out and touched the altar, my hand shaking involuntarily.

The instant my hand made contact with the altar, the wind-like sound was replaced by a sound that I can barely bring myself to describe. The screeching roar of metallic nails tearing down a blackboard, the roar of a lion played backwards, a thousand bows tearing badly against a thousand violin strings. So loud and so horrific was the sound that I dropped to my knees and covered my ears. I felt as though my eardrums might burst, the pressure on them so intense that my eyes watered and winced. My hands clasped against my ears, I looked up and saw a shadow rise along the rear wall of the church. Covering the statue image of our Lord on the Cross, covering his mother stood to one side in mourning, covering the angel that watched over both. The shadow was larger than anything inside the church that could possibly have been the source of it. And its shape -- dear God, its shape -- if I were to ask you to imagine the shadow of a million writhing snakes, or perhaps tentacles, that might bring something to your mind which is close to what I saw. I closed my eyes and joined the hideous noise with a scream of my own, and then all fell silent.

Tentatively, I removed my hands from my ears and got back to my feet. My entire body was shaking and I looked all about me for any sign of what I had just seen with all the caution of a nervous cat. I saw nothing. I heard nothing. Except... the first candle on the Advent Crown had gone out. I re-lit it immediately, and then quickly locked up the church and went home.

#

Tuesday 5th December

I lost most of Sunday afternoon, and the entirety of Monday, to my studies of Father Hirst's journal. I'd have lost much of today as well, were it not for a phone call reminding me of tea and cakes at Mrs Wedgeworth's house. Slightly flavourless as that cake may have been, it was a welcome distraction from the pages of that old journal. What can I say about it and still sound like a rational man? Well, it's clear that he was passionate about this village and its church. Like myself, it seems that he was not in fact a long-time resident of the village. He'd come here in his thirties, as I have myself, and stayed here until his death four decades later. He truly had loved the place.

In his time here, Father Hirst had studied much local history, and for want of a better term, folklore. Whilst the official doctrine of the Church is to disregard such things and replace old beliefs and superstitions with the practice of good, moral Christian worship, it's certainly true that it has been known to be flexible in such things. There are many priests in Ireland who would confess to a belief in fairies and still keep an iron frame around the doors of their houses, for instance, and many more who still partake of séances and the like. As for the village of Umberton, Father Hirst had discovered that it was not always quite so pleasant a place as it is now.

The Black Death, the somewhat colourful

name for the bubonic plague, had struck the village hard. Many of its families were lost, never to be replaced. The remaining ones abandoned their faith in God and turned instead to something else for protection. The exact name or nature of what this might have been, Father Hirst does not detail. In fact he seems to devoutly refuse to do so, as if identifying it might give it power. Nor does he say how well this new form of Faith performed in protecting the village from the plague. It's certainly true that enough survived to see the village through to a new area of prosperity in the years that followed, but how far this can be laid at the door of superstitious practices is probably open for debate. The plague subsided in many areas of England which never claimed to have turned to any Faustian bargain, after all.

Father Hirst detailed how the Church sought to re-establish itself in areas where its hold had loosened, and Umberton was one of them. The return of, as he describes it, The Light Of Christianity to the area appeared to have been welcomed by most. The practices of this new faith they'd adopted had apparently not settled easily with the village, whatever benefits it may have seemingly brought to them (if it indeed it had brought any at all.) So the new Church was built, and as Hirst writes, the Old Darkness was locked away beneath it. Sealed forever by the light of faith in God. The true God, to use his words, although personally I'm not sure such a term is necessary unless we accept that other beings might exist who claim divinity.

His writings over the year are mostly what you'd expect from a priest's journals, so I won't detail much more of the minutiae less my own journal become merely a copy of Hirst's. It is only in his later years, that he once again refers to the history of the village, and that's when the Crown is first mentioned. He believed a shadow was spreading within the church. That statement sent a chill down my spine, given my own experience at the altar. The decline in Church attendance had, to Hirst's mind, reduced the power of the place as a barrier against what came before. And in the period of the darkest month, December, the power of this -- whatever he believed it to be -- was at its peak. So he added further strength to the ritual of the advent crown, by keeping its light burning through the entire month. This, he believed, would suffice in making up the shortfall caused by the empty pews.

I have no reason to believe that Father Hirst was a man possessed of anything other than sound mind, right until the end. His writings always remain clear and concise at all times of the year except when he talks about the crown and its purpose. At the time of these writings, every year, it as though a desperate fury comes over him and he can think of naught else. I pity him, really, to have become so obsessed with a ritual of his own devising. And yet, I can say that as I sit here in daylight, in the comfort of the modern world, with no consequence. But all I need do is think back to my own experience in the church last Sunday, and a very real chill travels down my spine.

#

Sunday 10ᵗʰ December

I led the church service today, against Doctor's orders, despite having missed Mass on Friday. Father Lewis, lovely chap from the neighbouring village, retired now but still in good health, came over in his car and led the Mass for me. But today, I had to light the Crown. I couldn't bear not to. I should elaborate, as I have mentioned my health without explanation.

Around Thursday morning, I started to feel very weak, as though the strength had been stolen from my limbs. Next came a fever, then cold sweats, and finally an absolute inability to keep food or liquid in my body. Now, to contract the flu at this time of year hardly seems unusual, save for the fact that I have not been in contact with anybody else who seemed to be suffering from it. Rather it seemed as though the illness had manifested itself in me alone.

The strength of my symptoms grew worse as the day went on, until I could barely rise from my bed by the evening. As I lay in a feverish and sweat-covered state, I once again became consumed with the feeling that I was not alone in my house. The door to my bedroom was open, allowing me easy access to the bathroom along the hallway. In said doorway, I could see the shadow of a figure. No, not a shadow, for shadows are pressed against walls, floors and ceiling. Rather, this was a shadow as though detached from a surface. Clearly not a fully solidified image, but present nonetheless. This was not at all like the shadow I'd seen in the church, but instead vaguely humanoid. In my almost-delirious state I would have sworn that somebody was stood in the doorway. It seems simple to try and pass this off as a fever-dream, but the similar experience I had whilst in the loft was born under no such illness.

I stared at the shadow, finding it unnerving and yet somehow not terrifying in the way that the monstrous shade in the church had been. The right arm of the shape raised and pointed at me, then moved to the right as though pointing beyond the walls of the house. A voice came not directly from the shadow, but from all around me;

"It has gone out."

The icy chill that caused me to shudder violently cut through the fever and forced me from my bed. The shadow was gone as quickly as it had arrived, but fever-dream or not, I couldn't ignore its words. I felt compelled by them, as much in soul as in mind and body. Climbing from my bed, ignoring even the prospect of a quick bath to freshen me up, I dressed and dosed myself up with as much cold medicine as I could safely take, and walked to the church.

Putting one foot in front of the other was more effort than I can describe to you. More than just the illness, I felt as though something were actively trying to push me back with each footfall. I am aware of the ludicrous nature of this statement, but I can only document my own experience. At least some modicum of luck was on my side, however, in that I didn't encounter any parishioners on the short walk to the church. It wasn't simply that I didn't have the energy to talk with them, but also that I dare not be slowed in my purpose.

Arriving at the church, I locked the door behind me so that nobody might wander in and distract me. My eyes then turned immediately to the Advent Crown; it was unlit. I had somehow known that this was what I would find, and yet this prediction did nothing to quell the horror of the sight. Resting on the pews as I went, my strength abandoning me already, I staggered over to the crown. Opening the hollow section, I discovered that the paraffin well was bone dry. Of course it was, I was due to refill it today and my sickness had prevented me from coming to the church to do so. Was the subconscious reminder of this what gave form to the shadow in my doorway? That seems a logical conclusion, and yet it doesn't fit with what my mind is increasingly believing to be the case. Father Hirst wants me to keep that crown lit, and is informing me of this in whatever capacity that he remains able, wherever he may be.

Thankfully I had previously had the foresight to leave a bottle of liquid paraffin in the utility cupboard, so I took this now and refilled the crown. My hands shook, causing some of it to splash on my sleeve. I lit the first candle. Somehow, the flame flickered to the side and caught my sleeve, setting it alight. I furiously patted it out, burning my hand in the process. More and more, I felt as though I was beset by competing forces of unnatural origin. Father Hirst, who wanted me to light the crown, and something else, which wished to prevent this very act.

Once back home I called the doctor to come and see to my burned hand, and whilst there he also gave me some better flu medicine and ordered me to rest. I conceded and arranged for the Friday Mass to be taken care of, as I have previously explained. I felt well enough today that I took the Sunday service myself, which of course included the lighting of the second candle on the Advent Crown. However ridiculous it may sound, I will now ensure that they stay lit until Christmas Day, to be joined by the third and fourth candle as the ritual demands.

#

Sunday 17th December

I recovered from my illness around Wednesday and haven't really had the time to write in this journal since then as I was catching up on Church matters. I held Mass on Friday, which was busier than I expected but not as busy as I'd hoped. And today was the Sunday service followed by the lighting of the third candle of Advent. The final candle will be lit on Christmas Eve.

The lighting of the third candle went without incident. I don't know exactly what I was expecting to happen, but given the unusual events that have occurred since my owning of the ritual, I have suffered from a vague anxiety around it. This is concentrated largely around ensuring that the crown remains lit, which I have now done on a daily basis, but the anxiety rose to a crescendo when it came time to light the third candle. Even there in the midst of a (not exactly full, but still healthy) church congregation, I felt that creeping dread as I reached for the wick. Something was going to happen to prevent me from lighting it. Another illness, an accident, even the guided hand of one of the parishioners. Guided by what, I cannot say. Thankfully I was wrong in every regard.

You'd think this would fill me with relief, perhaps even a reassurance that the previous events were indeed the product of an ill mind and body, coupled with a fired-up imagination. I feel no such cause for celebration. Rather I now suffer from a creeping dread at the back of my mind, as though I am not out of the proverbial storm, but rather sat in the eye of it. As though my opponent is merely biding his time for one last push.

#

Sunday 24ᵗʰ December

I'm sat in the church as I write this. I've pulled a folding chair next to the spot where the advent crown hangs, and I sit with the paraffin bottle and box of matches ready to re-light it as often as required. It keeps going out. There is noise inside the church. Terrible, unnatural noise. And a howl that rises to a crescendo, one which has nothing to do with the snowy winds blowing through the shattered windows. I feel my mind may snap, and so I must write to stay focused.

The snow started on Friday evening just after Mass, and has not stopped since. It has fallen heavier as Sunday approached. Whilst the arrival of a heavy snowfall just before Christmas Day is welcome by many, I did not see it this way. I feel that at any other year, I would have joined the chorus of those sledding and building snowmen and enjoying the magic of the season. But I saw the snowfall as yet another barrier. The intention was for the snow to fall so heavy that I couldn't walk to the church for the Sunday Service. To barricade the door with such strong drifts that the church would be sealed. I know how this sounds, you must believe me that I know. But I am sure of it.

Whether there was indeed malicious intent behind the snow or not, it did not prevent me from getting to church this morning. Few made the journey, but I cannot really blame for this. With it being Christmas Eve and the downfall being so sudden, there has been no efforts to clear the

59

roads or walkways in the village, so conditions have become rather treacherous. There were fewer than ten of us in the church, but that was enough. As long as I was there to light the final candle of the advent crown, that was all that mattered. I believed, naively as I now understand it, that lighting the final candle would put an end to it. How foolish of me.

No sooner had the congregation left, the joy and light of their faith and celebration now departed from the church, that a draft blew through the church so fiercely that two of the candles on the crown went out. I re-lit them immediately, and was beset with an agonising cramp along my arm. I dropped the box of matches and clutched my shoulder, so blinding was the pain. I felt as though the limbs of an octopus were wrapped about it, clenching tighter with each second. Was this a heart attack? It was my left arm where the pain was felt, which is, I am led to believe, where the pain occurs during such an ailment. I didn't know what else to do, so I staggered to the altar and knelt before the cross, then prayed.

This act of prayer relieved the tension in my arm, as though whatever grasped it had been forced to let go. The rational part of my mind insists it is merely that I had calmed myself down, but at this point I don't know what to believe. For in the next moment, the entire church shook as though struck with a mighty blow of force. Not from above, however, but from below.

The advent crown swung wildly, and two of the candles went out. I got to my feet and ran to it, steadying it by hand and then re-lighting it. I checked the paraffin levels, and was assured it was still more than half full. I had become somewhat obsessive about not letting the fuel drop below a quarter, but nonetheless I couldn't help but check each time my eye met the slit where the fuel level could be seen. The church shook again, this time the altar being forced forwards down the steps with such a crash that I felt I might suffer a genuine heart attack this time. The golden cross skidded across the floor to my feet, and I instinctively picked it up and clutched it close to me. With my free hand I steadied the stand atop which sat the advent crown.

A sound of howling wind filled the church, as it had done with the lighting of the first candle, and once again I could detect its source. It was coming from where the altar had once stood. There was something below it, hidden in the floor. I wanted to move closer but I daren't leave my post. The crown couldn't be left unattended, for I feared this would be the end of me. The church shook again, and two of the windows broke inwards, the shards of coloured glass flying into the church. I was far enough away that I wasn't injured by the jagged projectiles, but I still watched in horror as those beautiful images were destroyed forever in a moment's violence.

Snow blew into the church, bringing with it the cold storm winds from outside to accompany the unnatural wind from within. I shielded the advent crown with my body and began to say the Lord's Prayer, over and over. After the seventh time through the prayer, the unnatural howling ceased, and even the snow blowing in from outside seemed to lessen. I took this moment to furiously write this entry in my diary, lest my sanity abandon me, and I remember these events in future as not having truly occurred. I must document them, I cannot allow whatever this presence is to fool me into thinking I have merely lost my grip on reality. Its attack has ceased for the moment, but this is, once again, the eye of the storm. It wants the light of the crown to be blown out, and it wants to return to this world. I cannot let it. I know that, if I keep the flames lit until the midnight hour, when the holy day is upon us, then all will be well. I must keep the crown lit.

#

December 26th

I was able to gain access to the church on Christmas Day morning at approximately 12:05 am, after clearing heavy snowdrifts from the door. The reason for my visit was that I was enquiring after the safety of Father Leopold Dunley, Priest of Umberton's Church. He hadn't been seen since the morning service on Christmas Eve, and phone calls to both his home and the church had gone unanswered. When the few devout souls who braved the weather for the traditional Midnight Mass arrived at the church, they found the doors barricaded from the inside and several of the windows broken. At that point the police were called.

I was able to climb into the church through the use of a stepladder and one of the broken windows, as I was unable to force the doors against whatever weight was set against them. Once I got inside I saw that several heavy wooden pews had been uprooted and pushed against the door. The altar was upturned and fallen at the top of the church aisle, just at the base of the steps, and broken coloured glass littered the floor from the windows. Snow drifts had formed inside against the walls where the snow had blown in. Where the altar had once stood, a hidden trapdoor covered in engraved scripture was now open, revealing a small stone chamber that was six foot

63

wide by six foot long by six foot deep. Nothing was to be found within the chamber, except for the black slimy residue of some oil-like substance. A trail of this same substance could also be seen stretching from the edge of the trapdoor, down the steps to the centre of the aisle. The blackish trail stopped at the exact point where I found Father Dunley.

The priest was unconscious, and his body was extremely cold. I was able to rouse him, and immediately took my jacket and wrapped it around his shoulders. I quickly went back to my car and radioed for an ambulance. When I returned, he was on his feet. I told him to sit down on one of the pews, and he complied. I asked him what had happened, and what was the origin of the black oil-like substance that had left a trail from the secret trapdoor to where I had found him. He explained that the chamber had been a store of very old, and very valuable, wine and liquor from centuries past when smugglers would hide their wares by bribing the church. Apparently some local reprobates broke into the church to steal the wine, and found the Priest already in attendance. They attacked him, barricaded the church door, and escaped via the broken windows, spilling some of the liquor in the process.

I will state for the record that I do not believe this to be the full truth. The black liquid does not look like liquor to me, but has more in common with the trails left by a slug or snail. If it isn't liquor, though, I have no idea what else it might be. Father Dunley's explanation of the attack also doesn't add up. He says they struck him in the back of the head, yet he has no visible wound there or any evidence of concussion. What he *does* have are several burns on his arms and neck as though ropes were wrapped around his person. I also found traces of that same black liquid around these burns. I believe Father Dunley is protecting somebody, a theory that was reinforced when he stated emphatically that he didn't wish to pursue the matter or seek to press charges. His reasoning for this was that the young men were clearly desperate, and at Christmas we must remember the Lord's message of forgiveness.

My final comments on this matter are regarding the character of Father Dunley himself. I've only met him on one or two occasions before this incident, but I still feel as though the attack affected him more than he claimed. I fully suspect he was in shock and not yet himself, despite his insisting otherwise as I removed the barricade and took him from the church, but he seemed very out of sorts. His voice, his mannerisms, even the way he smiled, none of it seemed like he was quite right. This feeling was further cemented in my mind when, as we left, I pointed to the broken Advent Crown that lay on the stone floor. It has become well known in the village how seriously Father Dunley has taken on the old tradition of Father Hirst's Advent, so his reaction to the broken crown was surprising to me. I asked him if he would be getting it repaired in time for next year's

Christmas period. His response was that he would not, and that the crown *"no longer served any purpose"*.

The End

Santa's Claws
By
Mark Allan Gunnells

He comes when everyone is asleep,
Down the chimney and through the house he
creeps.

Dressed in red with a yellowing beard,
He's the sum of all I've ever feared.

He brings me gifts I don't desire—
A talking doll that is a liar,

A teddy bear with a corpse's eyes,
A pair of shoes that aren't my size.

He leaves them underneath the tree,
Whose needles brown instantly

And fall to the floor, dead as rot.
They say he's jolly, but I know he's not.

He's as bitter as the winter's wind,
A hermit with only trolls for friends.

Each year he stands at the foot of my bed.
"Have you been good this year?" he says,

Laughing all the while because
If the answer's "no" he shows his claws.

His wicked laugh can bring me to tears
As I wonder, "Have I been good enough this year?"

Santa's Gift
By
Mark Allan Gunnells

Sam wasn't happy.

This was all Carol's fault. If he hadn't had to get her that diamond bracelet for Christmas, he wouldn't be here right now.

To be fair, it wasn't as if she'd asked for the bracelet, but she'd been berating him for the past twelve months about last year's gift. He thought she'd love a new microwave, but he'd been wrong. *Very* wrong. So he had to do something super special this year to make up for it. Thus this crappy part-time job so he could afford that bracelet.

Taking a deep breath and readjusting his itchy beard, he walked out of the back storeroom. The dozens of kids who had gathered in a single-file line behind the rope barricade gasped collectively and started chanting, "Santa! Santa! Santa!"

"Jesus Christ," Sam mumbled under his breath as he took his seat on the chair that looked like some kind of throne. Though he certainly didn't feel like a king.

For three weeks he'd been working as a department Santa, and he'd been kicked, smacked, candy canes stuck in fake beard, spit on, and one squirmy little boy had even peed on him. But tonight was his last night. Just had to get through a few more hours of a parade of brats taking turns on his lap and then he was free. And hopefully out of the doghouse with Carol.

The first kid was a little girl who wanted a remote control car. *Future lesbian*, Sam thought and couldn't help but chuckle to himself. A boy who wanted some new Wii games, a 12 year old who wanted a cell phone, a set of twins who sat one on each knee, one of which wanted a Kindle and the other a Nook. Sam couldn't help but muse at how different things were these days compared to when he was a kid.

About an hour into his shift, a little girl wearing a big hooded parka shook off her mother's hand and came marching up to Sam, clamoring onto his lap. Her face was twisted with determination. A girl with a mission.

"Well hello, dear," Sam said in his best Santa voice. "What is your name?"

"Shouldn't you already know it? I mean, if you're really Santa."

With an internal sigh, Sam looked back toward the rope where the girl's mother waited. The woman mouthed "Susie."

"Why, you're little Susie, aren't you? You've just grown so much since last year that I hardly recognized you."

"Or maybe you're just going senile."

"Susie," the girl's mother exclaimed from her place behind the rope. "Don't be rude."

Sam wasn't in the mood for this, but he forced out a "Ho ho ho. That's okay, Santa is getting a bit up there in age."

Susie folded her arms and smirked at Sam. She couldn't have been more than ten, but her expression, mannerisms and the way she talked made her seem older. "Do you sometimes get kids mixed up?"

"What do you mean?"

"Like maybe you give gifts meant for one kid to another?"

Sam just shook his head, confused, and looked back to the girl's mother who shrugged.

"Let me refresh your memory, Santa," Susie said. "Last year I sent you a letter asking for a bicycle and I didn't get one. I knew my mother would never be able to afford one, so I wrote the letter myself, took a stamp from my mother's purse, and mailed it all without telling her. That way she'd be as surprised as me. And I was surprised alright, surprised when I didn't get a bike."

Damn, here he was so close to freedom and he had to get stuck in this sticky situation. "Look, Susie, you have to understand—"

"Is this where you start offering up excuses. Maybe the letter got lost in the mail; maybe an elf made a mix-up; maybe my bike fell out of the sleigh over the Atlantic Ocean. Just save it. You're a fraud, and you deserve to be punished."

"Susie, please just—"

"Santa, I think it's time I gave you a gift," Susie said, reaching into her parka. "It's something Daddy left behind when he left."

Sam heard the screams of the crowd before he saw the gun in the little girl's hand.

The End

White Oleanders
By
Steven Stacy

"Turn this one up!" Lowri yelled from the backseat of the Subaru Forester SUV. Ryan did as she asked for once and turned the radio station up - 'Walking in a Winter Wonderland' blasted out, and Lowri and her best-friend Jennifer started singing at the top of their voices. "In the meadow we could build a snowman!" The boys looked at each other in the front seats and rolled their eyes, although Johnny couldn't help but smile to himself.

It was the first holiday the four of them had gone on together. When Ryan told Lowri he was taking her to Courchevel for a Christmas skiing holiday, Johnny had made up his mind that he'd work all Summer to earn the money to take Jennifer and go with them. Ryan never had to worry about cash, his parents were loaded, and they didn't mind letting their only child have whatever he wanted. Lowri was also lucky, in the fact that being Ryan's girlfriend meant she got to join him wherever he went.

Lowri smiled from ear to ear. The scenery was beautiful; breathtakingly beautiful. Her entire world had changed since meeting Ryan, and she thanked God that out of all the girls in University he had wanted to date her; had chased her, in fact. Not that she couldn't have her pick, but it was always nice when the guy made the first move.

"Okay, enough!" Ryan said, annoyed, and turned the radio down.

"Hey!" Jen said, shocked. "We were enjoying that."

"Ryan don't be such a kill joy," Lowri cried, clearly embarrassed. Her dimples faded, and she folded her arms in annoyance.

"Let them have their fun," Johnny chimed in. Ryan gave him an exasperated look.

"Don't you start! I need to concentrate on these mountain roads, my parents will kill me if I wreck another car," Ryan said, turning his eyes back to the snow-covered road.

"It's so pretty," Jen sighed, relaxing back into her seat and looking out the window at the snow-capped mountains and the pretty, European style, villages all lit up for Christmas.

"I think I'd have had a fever, from excitement, if I'd seen this as a little girl," Lowri said to Jen.

"I can't believe we're seeing it at all," Jen said, still in awe.

"Oh my God! Look, it's the Coca-Cola Santa truck," Johnny pointed out. Lowri leaned forward between the two front seats, the huge Coca-Cola truck with an image of Santa taking a swig of the brown liquid was parked by the side of the road. It had the multi-coloured lights situated all around the giant vehicle and looked out of place just sat there.

"It's filthy," Lowri said with surprise, as her eyes examined the mud all over the sides of the truck and especially on the front driver's door and even the wind-screen. It had also fallen into disrepair, brown rust appeared in patches and the wonky exhaust was letting out an ugly, smoky cloud. Immediately, Ryan put his foot down on the accelerator. "What are you doing?" Lowri asked, a bad feeling in the pit of her stomach erupting.

"Hey buddy, you're going way too fast. . ." Johnny looked towards Ryan, who wasn't stopping. As they got closer to the huge lorry, Lowri could see that it was dented from accidents and even some of the multi coloured bulbs had blown.

"Maybe he needs help? A blown tire perhaps," Jen suggested. Ryan continued to speed ever closer. "Ryan, slow down! You're going to get us killed! Plus, you could total the car."

Ryan wasn't listening though, and a smirk had spread over his handsome face. He pushed a button to let his window down and, ignoring his three friends who were yelling in protest, he swerved towards the truck sending a torrent of slush and snow up and all over the driver's door and window. Ryan leaned his head out and yelled, "Wash your vehicle, ya filthy animal!"

"Jesus! Are you crazy?" Lowri asked, checking her seatbelt was done up properly.

"Ryan would you at least put the window up, it's freezing," Jen moaned, pulling her padded gilet closed. The window started going up.

"Some Santa," Ryan said laughing. "The filthy git." Johnny joined in on the laughter, and eventually even the girls giggled. "Hey, you wanted me to get festive – there's a 'Home Alone' joke for you!"

"You could've got us in trouble though," Lowri said, mock hitting the top of Ryan's arm.

"My SUV, my rules!" Ryan stated flatly. None of the four saw the fairy lights burst into colour as the Christmas-Cola-truck roared into movement behind them.

"Your boyfriend is crazy," Jennifer said in a hushed tone, pushing her long dark hair back. Lowri attempted a weak smile, but her brown eyes couldn't hide her embarrassment. She hated Ryan's constant need to show off, especially in front of Jen who was so practical.

It seemed slightly odd that Lowri now considered Jennifer a friend, and a very close friend too, when they had barely known each other a year. Lowri could pin-point the day it had blossomed; from them being acquaintances (who had boyfriend's that were best-friends), to them actually bonding. One of the girls from class had been having a go at Lowri in the changing rooms.

"Look at you, walking around like your God's gift. Ryan Hardy wouldn't have looked at you if you didn't go around showing off what the rest of us choose to keep covered up." Jennifer had been in one of the lady's stalls and had just seemed to appear from nowhere.

"You're just jealous, Marion. Besides, if I had a killer body like Lowri, I'd show it off too." Marion Childs had shut her mouth after that, and Lowri had been so grateful to Jen. No one had ever stuck up for her like that before, not even a family member. Jennifer had been respected in University, for her intellect and the way she carried herself. Lowri had dropped out not long after, she couldn't afford it. Not even working full time. Besides, she wasn't really an academic. Ryan had not been pleased. She knew her looks were her meal ticket, and so she had concentrated on them. She'd done a few commercials after being picked up by an agency. She'd then landed a toothpaste campaign and the money from that had allowed her to move out of the family home. Ryan had been proud of her *then*, and she had been proud of herself, more importantly.

Lowri was too busy chatting to Jen to notice the sound consciously for a while, but when the conversation broke, she could hear a huge thunderous engine. She turned instinctively and looked out the rear window. The Christmas-Coca-Cola-truck was zooming behind them, it's working lights twinkling. "Omigod, Ryan, behind us!"

"Shit!" Ryan said, glancing in the rear-view-mirror. He floored the gas pedal to stop the Coca-Cola-truck going straight into the back of them. They were all now craning their necks to watch as the truck which was billowing dirty grey smoke wouldn't quit. "What the hell is he feeding that thing?" Ryan said. They were already doing ninety, and if it wasn't for Ryan's expert driving the truck would've tail-ended them.

"There!" Johnny yelled, pointing to a fork in the road which led to a gas-stop and shopping-complex. Ryan manoeuvred the SUV, bumped and demolished a heap of snow, before making the turning. "Well done buddy, that was some brilliant driving," Johnny said relaxing back into his seat as the SUV screeched to a slow halt. Johnny watched as the truck disappeared around a hard bend on the mountain road, it's billows of smoke wafting behind it.

"What the fuck was that guys problem?" Ryan asked.

"I'm guessing he didn't like your Christmas joke," Jen cracked, clearly pissed off. They were receiving curious looks from passers-by, and Ryan gave them the finger. "Look, there's toilets. I need to pee," Jen whined before opening her door and racing towards the complex.

"Actually, I need to go myself," Johnny admitted. "And I wouldn't mind a burger after all of that." Ryan sighed heavily and started to park outside the complex. "Look, they have a

McDonald's!" Johnny laughed. "I bet they have a McDonald's at the bloody North Pole."

"You can ask Santa when you get there, if we ever do! We're losing time by stopping constantly," Ryan moaned. Lowri leant forward and massaged Ryan's shoulder's, trying to ease his bad mood.

"Stop worrying so much babe, we've still got plenty of time."

The four of them got out and made their way towards the rest-stop, which was lit up and decorated for Christmas beautifully. The entire roof was covered in snow with a false Santa waving from his sleigh made of dancing reindeer, icicles hung down all over a wooden porch, and there were fairy-lights all over the entire building. Lowri got out and stared at the giant Christmas tree which was covered in white and blue lights with a beautiful Angel atop it. She had never seen anything so pretty, it was like going to Hogwarts, she thought giddily. The snow was coming down heavily and their footprints had disappeared by the time they had reached the shopping complex.

Lowri noticed a vending machine just outside the building. "I'm gonna buy a drink, I'll catch you up," she smiled. Ryan mumbled some response and Johnny was too busy rushing towards the toilets to notice. She walked past a group of boys carrying ski-boards and received a few wolf whistles, to which she smiled and blushed.

"You're the Colgate-White girl!" A boy with bleached dreads said stopping in his tracks. "Can we have a picture with you?" He asked. His friends were gathering around and one guy with short dark hair gave her a wink. Before she knew it, she was posing in the centre of the group with them, in front of a camera mounted on a selfie stick. She did her Colgate smile and a peace sign with her fingers. She just hoped she didn't look as red as she felt. They all thanked her and moved on.

Lowri carried on to the drinks dispenser and punched in the code for a can of Pepsi. She bent down and fetched it. She opened the can and glugged some of the syrupy liquid back. Suddenly, an engine revved twice, loudly, behind her. She jumped, spilling some of the contents down her grey sweater. She saw the multi-coloured lights reflected in the glass of the dispenser before she turned around and saw the Coca-Cola-Christmas-truck behind her, parked in the parking lot. She squinted but couldn't see the driver through the flurry of snow. It was almost like a wolf whistle, if machines had feelings. The headlights came on full beam, blinding her for a second. Her hand went up to block the light instinctively. She squinted and turned away, "shit!" She walked quickly back toward the entrance of the rest-stop, regretting buying fingerless gloves, as her fingers froze against the icy can and the freezing weather. Her flares were also getting gradually damper as they soaked up the water and slush; she wouldn't tell Ryan though because he'd already complained about her outfit several times, finally forcing her into her three-quarter length coat on top of all the other layers. She must admit he *had* been spot-on about the cold weather. They were only travelling in the Jeep though, as far as she was concerned; and the heating was on full-blast constantly.

She nervously looked behind her again, the lights were now off on the truck, and she found the doorway to the café they were all sat inside. It was busy and smelt of cinnamon and chocolate. Lowri found them locked in the middle of a serious conversation, and all had huge mugs of hot chocolate with marshmallows and squirty cream on top in front of them. Lowri sat down, and Ryan pushed her hot chocolate towards her without looking at her. "No, no, you're wrong! Father Christmas was this skinny dude dressed in green and he's real! He's a Saint or something," Johnny was explaining, while looking slightly flushed.

"Yes, Saint Nicholas of Myra," Jennifer said as if talking to a bunch of idiots. Lowri looked outside and wondered if the driver had followed her into the busy café. *How did he get here so fast?* She shivered and took a sip of her warm hot chocolate. *He must've done a U-Turn to follow them.* She popped the marshmallow in her mouth and rolled her eyes, waiting for her friends to shut up. She started to speak, but Ryan held his hand up to stop her. She sighed loudly and crossed her arms, impatiently. Jen gave her a '*don't let him treat you like that*' look.

"Who gives a shit?" Ryan said and then took a bite from his burger.

"Yeah, but the point is, Coca-Cola made the guy fat and cute. Coca-Cola gave him the red suit, it should be green," Johnny insisted.

"Correct," Jen stated, like it was the answer in a quiz.

"That Christmas lorry is outside, and he is seriously pissed!" Lowri blurted out.

"What the fuck is that arsehole up-to?" Ryan muttered under his breath and looked over his shoulder, past his padded ski-jacket and outside. "What did he do?"

"He scared the shit out of me, I was drinking, and he blasted his horn twice right behind me. It made me jump out of my skin."

"You mean he followed us?" Jennifer looked concerned. Lowri immediately regretted telling her boyfriend as she saw Ryan's face change from carefree to furious. He started to get up, leaving his half-eaten burger, and pushing past Jen.

"Are you okay?" Johnny asked Lowri, placing his hand on her arm.

"I'm fine, just a bit shook up."

"I think you pissed off someone with road-rage, honey," Jen smiled sarcastically. "Not that Ryan would know *anything* about road-rage, of course... "

"I'm gonna teach that cocky bastard a lesson," Ryan said as he started storming towards the doors.

Jen sighed, pushing her food away and getting up to follow him, along with Johnny. Lowri ran after them. "Ryan, leave it alone!" she hollered. But he was already outside walking towards the flashing Christmas lights in the parking lot.

"Hey, you need to pay bill," a waitress said in pidgin English, stopping Jen and Lowri.

"We'll be right back, I promise!" Lowri said, palms up.

It was freezing outside, and Lowri felt ridiculous not wearing the ski-jacket Ryan had bought her. The wind whipped her short-bleached bob into her eyes, and the children's daisy chain she'd been wearing in her hair flew off in the gust. She could just make out Jen's luminescent pink ski outfit, and she ran after it, chastising herself for not bringing her snow goggles. Of course, *they* all had money and she was relying on the kindness of Ryan. She was already feeling like a free-loader. "Jen!" she screamed, now getting slightly scared that she couldn't see a hand in front of her. The snow storm had increased suddenly, and the flashing Christmas lights unexpectedly went out on the truck.

Ryan pounded on the side of the cola truck; he'd found easily. "Well then, come out and fight you fucking chicken! Or can you only pick on girls?" He looked around, even with his goggles he could hardy see a few feet ahead and fear trickled down his spine. He pounded on the door with his fist. "Hey!" he screamed again. That was when the lorry door flew open and smashed into his face, dislodging two teeth and knocking him out. Ryan, not knowing what hit him, went down, unconscious, in a puff of snow and a splatter of blood.

Jen didn't see the figure rapidly approaching her from behind, she was lost. The snow storm had completely turned her around. She kept bumping into vehicles. The figure advanced quickly and as a hand gripped her shoulder, she turned around with a shriek, which got lost in the storm. "Oh my God, Lowri, I thought it was that guy from the Coca-Cola lorry! Have you seen Johnny or Ryan?"

"No, I was lucky to see you! Can we go back to the S.U.V and wait for them, I'm freezing? We're not going to find them in this storm anyway."

"Fine. . . I'm not chasing some testosterone filled idiot, no offence," Jen added, turning back.

"He's not usually like that, he was just. . ."

"Showing off?" Jen quipped, finishing Lowri's sentence for her. "You should really stop sticking up for him Lowri, you could do much better. . ." Jen stopped short. "Someone's gone into the back of us!" Jen shouted, reaching the SUV first. "Oh my God, it's been rammed," Jennifer alleged, looking through her snow goggles at the rear-side of the vehicle. She slammed the jeep's boot down which was open ajar, and it closed, luckily. Next, she got down on her knees and searched for the keys, which Ryan had placed underneath the SUV in a magnetic holder, and thankfully they were still there. Both girls got in either side of the vehicle. The leather was freezing under Lowri's bottom, as she pulled the door shut. "Do you think I should risk the engine?" Jen asked, looking at the emergency radio that had been destroyed with trepidation. The radio suddenly burst on and both girls jumped – 'Tis the season, it's always the real thing. . .' Jen turned it off.

"It's either that or freeze to death," Lowri said, holding herself and shivering. Jen started the Jeep and it came alive, pumping hot air out at a rate of knots.

"Thank God for small mercies," Lowri said warming her hands.

"I cannot believe you wore fingerless gloves to go skiing," Jen laughed at the bright red fingertips poking out of the black lace. Lowri looked at herself and started to laugh, just little giggles which batted back and forth, at first. Pretty soon both girls were doubled up in a hard belly-laugh. Of course, Lowri was trying to get Jen to stop by putting her hand on her shoulder, arm, leg. But all this just made Jen laugh harder when she saw the glamorous eighties-Madonna-style gloves in the middle of a snow storm, with pink frozen, fingertips poking out.

Suddenly the door burst open. Both girls screamed in unison. It was Johnny. He had blood on his face and hands, he looked like he was deep in shock; his bottom lip was quivering, and it was a pale shade of blue. He just sat there for a few moments in silence as both girls stared at him. Blood dripped from his nose and landed on the white snow of his trousers. Lowri couldn't resist. . . she'd waited longer than was necessary to ask, in her opinion. "Johnny. . . where's Ryan?" she said it as calmly and gently as possible, while placing a hand on his icy snow-jacket.

"He just disappeared," he whispered in shock; his words stoic and quiet.

"Where's the blood from?" Jen asked.

"I couldn't make it out properly through the snowstorm, but I tried to reach Ryan who was unconscious in the back of the truck."

"But you both play rugby, couldn't you tackle him to the ground, or something?" Jen asked gently. She had her hand on his, the one with no blood on, Lowri noticed.

"I couldn't see *anyone*, but the van door knocked me over, like the wind took hold of it or something. . .busted my nose," Johnny said, still staring forward in a daze. His dark eyes, haunted. "when I woke up the truck was gone."

Lowri took her phone out, "I'm calling the police," she said defiantly.

The police came almost immediately, and Lowri noticed from the gleam of all the lights and little scenes, that it was a full moon when they were leaving. They had guided them back to the café and had interviewed them. They didn't seem to be taking the thing as seriously as Lowri hoped, saying Ryan could've wondered off or got lost in the storm. It didn't really get them *anywhere*, except that the police were now looking out for a grubby looking Christmas Coca-Cola-truck. They'd let them know when they heard anything. They were told to continue to their hotel and wait for news.

Lowri felt lonely and lost without Ryan beside her, he'd always looked out for her since they'd first started going out. He'd asked her out last year in University with a bunch of white oleanders' in his hands for her, and everything had been better ever-since. Plus, she didn't feel so lonely. Loneliness was a *huge* issue for Lowri, she was a very anxious person and only medication helped her battle it. She looked over at Jennifer and Johnny, hand in hand, walking just ahead of her and felt a pang of jealousy. Suddenly the parking lot lit up, and a female voice came over the tannoy with a crackle. "We're sorry the parking lot lights have been out; this storm has come out of nowhere. We're trying to rectify the problem." *It was him*, Lowri thought, *the lunatic in the lorry*. She knew this wasn't rational, but she felt it in her gut.

In the newly replaced SUV, no-one said anything, and Jennifer drove, as Johnny was still in shock and Lowri was still too upset. Insurance had given them a replacement hire car when Lowri paid for the damages to the original with Ryan's card. He'd left his wallet on the table, inside the restaurant. She was still crying now, silently in the back seat, feeling sorry for herself and wondering if Ryan was okay while looking at his driver's licence photo. Their vehicle approached a railway crossing and had to stop, as a large barrier came down to stop them moving any further with a series of beeping noises.

"It was just a prank, I don't understand how someone could take it this far," Lowri said, and raked her hands through her hair, full of stress.

"People have been murr – *attacked* – for far less, Lowri," Johnny rationalised, always the voice of reason. "Try not to worry, you know Ryan is more than capable of looking after himself." The revving started somewhere in the back of her mind, far off, as traffic usually does. Then it was so close that all three of them leapt in their seats. Lowri looked behind to see that the Cola-Cola-truck was behind them, and worse still, Ryan had been chained to the grill, the chains in a criss-cross fashion; holding him in place. He looked like he'd been clocked on the skull, his head was bloodied.

Plus, he had a split lip. Lowri undid her seatbelt and went to open her door, as Johnny pressed the automatic lock down.

"You're not going out there!" he told her from the front seat, with more authority than she'd ever heard from Johnny's voice. He was looking over his shoulder, as was Jen at the sight behind them. After failing to open the door several times, Lowri scooted up towards the rear-window and looked out.

"Ryan!" she screamed. "Ryan!" her hand pressed against the back window. "We have to help him!" Suddenly the lights came on, full beam again, and blinded the three friends momentarily. Lowri dropped her head and covered her eyes trying to blink away the blossoms of light, which turned into white oleander's. There was a monstrous groan which sounded like Ryan, and she looked up immediately.

"We're moving!" Johnny shouted in horror. The truck was slowly pushing their SUV towards the blocked off railway track. Only Lowri noticed it was crushing Ryan's legs at the same time.

"Somebody *do* something!" Lowri yelled. Jen grabbed the break and pulled the stick back, trying to halt the tires which were now skidding against the snow. Ryan's legs had become a blurred mess of gore on the back window. "Drive forward!"

"I can't, there's a train coming!" Jen cried.

"Then let me out so I can help him, for God's sake!"

"Johnny. . ." Jen said looking at him with bright, terrified eyes, which pleaded with him to act.

"Stay here!" he ordered to the two girls before grabbing a crow bar which he'd hidden beside his seat, after taking it from the trunk. "Be careful, and don't wait for me," he hesitated looking back at Jennifer. "I love you, Jen," he said softly.

"Right back at you," she said, unable to say the words, knowing she was close to tears. Lowri watched as Johnny got out and started attacking the truck with the crow bar. Then he stopped and started to investigate something, a padlock on the chains which were holding Ryan in place. The two boys were communicating with each other when swiftly, the truck burst forward and slammed into the back of the SUV. The SUV jolted forward, causing both girls to scream. Ryan also screamed, and Lowri heard a bone break against the shattering thick glass, as the vehicles collided. Then she fell back between the two front seats, jerking her head backwards and causing her neck to strain; the cords grinding. Jennifer cried out as she jolted forward, the seatbelt winding her. Then the truck continued to push the SUV forwards. Johnny was aiming the crowbar now completely and utterly at the padlock holding Ryan atop the grill.

"Lowri, Lowri, get up! I need you to drive," Jen said, her voice weak and raspy. "I feel faint, I can't bloody breathe." Jennifer didn't look well; her face was a ghastly shade of white and she had a bloodied nose. Lowri couldn't believe this was happening, it was like some ghastly nightmare. She scrambled up into the driver's seat beside Jen and massaged her neck with one hand as she started the car with the other. "Put your seatbelt on!" Jen snivelled. Lowri did as Jennifer asked, when all of a sudden, the radio autotuned into a musical commercial ditty.

"*The Holidays are coming, holidays are coming, coming for everyone. . .*" Jen hit the radio power button angrily and turned it off.

"Just a coincidence," Jen said, confirming it as much to herself as to Lowri, as she sat back into the passenger seat. Lowri nodded and went to put her foot down.

"It's a Manual!" Lowri said, shocked. "I can only drive automatic," she said, hitting the steering wheel desperately. The Jeep was already crashing through the controlled crossing arms, the wood splintered and snapped. The light was on red to both girl's horror, they were being pushed onto the train-track. The SUV went up and down as it was forced over the thick metal beams. Jennifer tried to stay calm as she fiddled with her seatbelt, which she'd managed to force in backwards. "I'm going to move the stick, just put your foot down gently each time I say," Jen instructed, smearing her bloodied nose across the top of her lips.

"Okay, okay," Lowri said, trying to keep her mind on the task at hand.

"Right, first we're going into first, so - "Jen's voice got cut off as the radio started up again, this time at full blast. '*Holiday's refreshments what they bring, tis the season, watch out, look around, something's coming.*' Jen smashed the radio knob angrily with her hand and turned the sound to mute. She moved the stick into first gear. "Now put your foot down slowly," Jen repeated, her voice shaking. Lowri saw the light start flashing red, and adrenaline spiked in her stomach. She did as Jen instructed, probably a little too quickly, as the SUV made a terrible groaning sound. Lowri looked in the rear-view mirror to see it covered with dark blood. She could hear the train coming, and to her left she saw a beautiful, old fashioned choo-choo train, covered in Christmas lights, rounding a bend and coming right towards them.

"Oh my God, oh my God. . ." Lowri said hitting the steering wheel with the palm of her hands.

"Calm down and concentrate," Jen instructed. "Ease your foot down slowly," she said sternly. Lowri did as she was told; this time pushing her foot down as gently as possible. Jen moved the vehicle into second and the car started toward the second barrier. Lowri's head was in a flurry of thoughts, her eyes kept flashing back to the mirror where she could now see nothing but blood, she could hear the train vastly approaching and the SUV was starting to rumble on the tracks. "That's good," Jen said, her voice shaking. "We're going to have to ram the barrier." Jen moved the stick into third and the vehicle slammed against the second barrier, jolting both girls forward. She moved them quickly into reverse, as a horn from the fast approaching train blasted through the darkening sky. They flew backwards before Lowri slammed on the break. Jen quickly moved the stick into fourth and the gears cried out as Jen said "now!" and Lowri floored the gas pedal. The vehicle flew forward and smashed through the second barrier, but it barely got through and the train hit the back of the speeding car, sending it into a tailspin. Lowri screamed and closed her eyes as the car started to whirl around. Then her head hit something, and everything white went black.

When Lowri came around a few minutes later, she was hanging upside down, her seatbelt holding her in place. The Jeep had flipped. She looked over to Jennifer, who seemed to be unconscious. Both air-bags had deployed, but because of their position it was resting on their chests. "Jen! Jen, wake up!" Lowri screamed at her friend as her hands reached for the carpeted floor. Jen stirred slightly, blood trickled from her mouth. Then Lowri heard a sound that made the entire of her spine prickle with fear; the truck's horn blew twice – alerting her that it was still there. "Shit!" Lowri whispered to herself. *What is wrong with this lunatic?* She undid her seatbelt and fell onto the roof of the vehicle. Then awkwardly manoeuvred herself onto her hands and knees, feeling crushed and claustrophobic. "Jen, wake-up. We're in trouble. . ." Lowri whispered. Then she slapped Jen's face, and Jen snapped awake with a hurried intake of breath.

"What happened?" Jen asked with a raspy voice.

"The jeep flipped over, the train clipped us," Lowri explained. "That maniac driving the crazy Christmas truck from hell is still out there."

"Press the SOS button." Lowri looked around and saw that in between a row of buttons where you could get an operator for instructions and advice for the best hotel in the area, there was a button saying SOS. Lowri pressed it as Jen fiddled with the button for her seatbelt which was jammed and wouldn't undo.

"What's your emergency?" A female voice asked.

"Help us please, our cars flipped over, and my friend is stuck," Lowri said, pulling on Jen's seatbelt with a frantic look of worry on her face.

"It's okay, stay calm Miss. May I take your name, and do you know your location?" The operator asked, her voice calm and reassuring.

"Please *help* us! I don't know where we are, we just crossed a train track. My name is Lowri

Lawrence, this is my boyfriend Ryan Hardy's Jeep."

Suddenly, the SUV was hit again from behind, and it skidded forward. Lowri fell on her side and Jen's head lurched backwards in a mass of dark hair. Lowri saw that the back window was shattered, and snow had poured into the back of the Jeep. She leaned over and grabbed a shard of glass. "There's a maniac trying to kill us, he ran us off the road and kidnapped my boyfriend," Lowri said, her bottom lip trembling with fear. She used the glass to start cutting through Jen's seatbelt, while also cutting the palm of her own hand.

"We're trying to locate your vehicle now via the GPS."

"Lowri, get out and get help," Jen insisted, placing her hand on top of Lowri's.

"No, I'm not leaving you," Lowri swore. As she continued to try and slice through Jen's seatbelt, but was mostly just succeeding in slicing through the palm of her glove and hand.

"I'm sorry I didn't catch that, we have located your destination though and paramedics - " Abruptly the operator was cut off as the truck slammed into their overturned vehicle again. Sending it spinning again across the snow. Lowri dropped the glass and shot forward, slamming her shoulder into the driver seat's headboard. She cried out in pain, before falling back on all fours. She took several deep breaths, her hair sticking in strands to her face.

"Go and get help, for God's sake Lowri," Jen demanded. "I'll kill you if you let that bastard kill us all," she laughed and closed her eyes.

"I'll come back for you," Lowri said trying to comfort Jen. She then kicked her right foot backwards, slamming her Dr. Martin boot into the Safe-Ty-Glass. It shattered and caved in slowly like a canopy. She slammed her boot again twice into it, shattering it completely. Then, she turned and started crawling out of the window when a wave of vertigo came over her. She didn't realise that they were precariously near the edge of the mountain road and the steep, rock-side drop. Her eyes went to the left where the truck was revving to ram them again. It would send the SUV over the mountain edge, no doubt. She looked back to Jennifer and saw that she was unconscious, her arms hanging down to the ceiling, motionless. *Small blessings.* She crawled out of the jeep, frantically trying to rush and feeling terrible for leaving Jen behind. The Safe-Ty-Glass fell around her as she crawled out. She got to her feet with a groan as the truck started for them again. She ran as fast as she could to the other side of the road and slammed into the snowy mountain as the truck careered into the SUV and sent it tumbling over the side of the mountain drop. The horn blasted three times. Lowri started racing along the snowy road, staying close to the mountain, her fingers on fire. An explosion shook the mountain and she fell to her knees. The SUV must've exploded. *Jennifer.* Poor Jennifer.

"Help! Somebody help me!"

Behind her, the Coca-Cola-truck was backing up fast. Then the blessed sound of sirens could be heard approaching. Her arms flew from side to side as she ran as fast as she could. Then she spotted an ambulance. Lowri glanced behind her and stopped abruptly; *the Christmas truck was gone*. She stared into the white-out, horrified and confused.

The ambulance had given her a thorough check and said that apart from some superficial cuts which they'd dressed; she was physically fine. The emotional damage was separate, and she had been given a mild sedative and a prescription she was told she could cash in her hotel (*how the other half lived.*) *Emotional damage. Well they could say that again, with bells on.* She could hardly believe this morning she had started out on cloud nine, with an amazing (*brutish*) boyfriend, and two good friends (*one good-friend and her nice boyfriend*). Now they were gone. Just like that, each one had been snuffed out. She felt exhausted, emotionally and physically. Her eyes kept shutting for a few seconds and then panic would jerk her awake; adrenaline stirred at the base of her spine. She wanted Ryan to comfort her.

She felt completely alone and couldn't wait to call her mother from the sanctuary of her hotel room. Mostly just to hear a kind voice that she recognised.

Lowri sat in the backseat of a police vehicle,

as the damn radio played 'Jingle bell rock' to which the officer was whistling along to. Lowri folded her arms, tears gently but constantly running down her face. She'd been questioned for over two hours and was now being driven to her hotel by Officer Crane; he was a well built, overweight man with a carefree smile which insinuated he knew something you didn't. He was dressed in a suit and thick winter coat; his tie was loose around his bulging collar. The hotel was at the top of the mountain, *with the best views*, Ryan had bragged. So, they were again on the mountain road to Lowri's distaste and concern. "Would you like a candy cane?" Officer Crane asked. He pushed it through the mesh metal and into her hand.

"Thanks," Lowri said with a weak smile.

"So, you really don't know why this guy was after you?"

"Nope," Lowri muttered, tears spilling down her face. *Not that I saw a guy*.

"I know it doesn't feel like it at the moment, but honestly, everything is going to turn out fine."

"Thanks. . ." Lowri whispered, chin down. "You know in the horror movies and the sci-fi thrillers, the women are always bad-assed, they handle the situation with strength. I... I didn't do that. I broke, and I panicked, because the truth is, I was scared."

"That's perfectly understandable," Officer Crane said kindly. "You probably went into

98

survival mode." Lowri nodded. "Can I just clear something up?" Lowri nodded again and wiped her nose. "You saw both your boyfriend, Ryan Hardy, and your best friend Jennifer Parker die." He paused.

"Yes."

"But your friend Johnny Watson just disappeared?" Crane asked with wonder.

"I told you, he got out of the vehicle when that damn Christmas truck pushed us onto the railway tracks. It was to try and help Ryan! We've been through this!" She leaned forward, placing her fingers through the mesh wire that separated her from the Officer. "if you're trying to insinuate. . ." Lowri's voice rose in anger, but then she trailed off. She was instantly distracted by the appearance of headlights in the rear-view mirror. Her eyes bugged. "What is that? Behind us?" Lowri asked, panic shading her voice. She turned to look out the back window.

"It's just another truck, we have them all the time at this time of year," Officer Crane reassured her. She could hear the engine gaining behind them and her adrenaline started to spike even more. It was dark and the blizzard hadn't died down so she could hardly see.

"The holidays are coming, the holidays are coming," the Coca-Cola advert burst onto the radio in a shocking blast, which caused Lowri to jolt with surprise.

"It's him," Lowri said with slow realization. "It's him!" she screamed.

Officer Crane put his foot down and started to slow the vehicle. "It's alright, you're perfectly safe. I know this mountain like the back of my hand. What makes you think it's the suspect?"

"Please, just trust me." The Cola chime continued on in the background, like the recording had skipped and was stuck on repeat.

"The holidays are coming; the holidays are coming."

"This damn radio channel must be busted," Crane muttered to himself as he pulled the police car over to the side of the road, and languidly changed the radio station.

"The holidays are coming; the holidays are coming." Crane and Lowri both did a double take at the radio, before Crane shut it off. "Maybe there are Gremlins!"

"Okay, I agree. . .that *was* a little strange, but please remain calm Miss Lawrence." Lowri stared with big glassy eyes at the radio, her mouth agape. She told herself for the fiftieth time that she didn't believe in the paranormal, that a truck couldn't be evil. It just wasn't possible. But then another voice, one she wanted to hide from, whispered back – *but what if it is the truck. Just the truck.* After all, she had seen no attacker, Johnny had seen no one at all.

Crane killed the engine and opened his door readying himself to get out. "What are you doing?" Lowri cried desperately. She tried the door to get out alongside him, but it was locked. "Let me out!" Her eyes flashed to the rear-view mirror; the truck was gaining fast.

"You're safe there, and you're under my protection," he got out of the vehicle and reached back in for his loudspeaker. Lowri undid her seatbelt and scooted over to the other side of the vehicle, unable to stop desperate whimpers escaping her mouth.

"Please, Jesus, I beg you Officer Crane," she said trying to speak calmly. "I just want to get out and stand behind you." She remembered her psychology class as Crane deliberated his answer. She calmed her voice. "Officer Crane, if that truck crashes into this vehicle then your *only* witness to three murders could die. You're a nice man, a *sensible* man. Officer Crane, you do not want to be the cause of my death."

He thought about it, weighing up the risks both ways. He pointed his finger at her through the glass. "You stay behind *me,* and you don't move a muscle. You got that?" He asked, clearly stressed.

"Yes Sir," Lowri said, wanting to scream for him to hurry up. He unlocked the car and she practically fell out of the door. She left the blanket that had been wrapped around her inside.

The night air was freezing, temperatures must've dropped significantly throughout the day; and the wind whipped her pale hair around her face. The snowy mountains around her were bathed in the red and blue flashing light of the police vehicle. Lowri hurried around Officer Crane as he readied his holster and picked up the microphone.

"Please stop your vehicle at once and pull over, this is the police," Officer Crane said over the static induced microphone. The truck was nearly upon them. Lowri could see the flashing Christmas bulbs also painting the snowy mountains different colours and started to back up. The crunch of snow under her boots sounded quite cathartic. The Cola Christmas truck was still racing towards them. "Stop your vehicle now or I'll shoot!" Crane screamed into the microphone.

"It won't stop!" Lowri predicted ominously. She was still backing away.

Crane aimed his gun at the truck. It was far too close for comfort and within a minute would crash into them. "Get to the other side of the road," he shouted over his shoulder to Lowri. She simply shook her head.

"It's me that it wants!" Lowri screamed back. She realised with a gasp, and a wave of vertigo, that she was standing right next to the mountain drop, a staggered, snow coloured, vertical drop, that over-looked one of the Christmas villages. She forced herself to stay near the edge as Crane shot. He took out one of the trucks tyres and shot the windshield, shattering it. Lowri could see no-one driving in the darkness. The truck kept coming. Crane shot out the other front tyre this time, and the truck started to lose its momentum and started snaking, going from left to right.

"Run!" Crane screamed as the truck was about to strike, despite its zig-zagging style, it was still going after Lowri. Crane moved fast for a guy his size and age, and managed to jump to the right, just avoiding the truck. Next, the truck slammed into the police vehicle and sent it spinning out of the way and towards the mountain road. Lowri looked behind her once more and then the truck appeared suddenly. She screamed and disappeared from Crane's sight and the top of the mountain. The truck followed, falling in stiff movements, first the head, then the body fell afterwards; sliding down with the sound of screaming metal against rock.

Crane got up on his bruised knees and forced himself to run. He raced over to the edge. "Lowri! Lowri!" he screamed, his booming voice echoing in the mountains. His eyes scanned the mountain, the lorry lay at the bottom, on its side, oil spilling out, and looking like the toy-trucks his kids played with.

"Pull me up!" Lowri called with a hoarse voice. She was clinging to the rock side, her fingers dug deep into the snow and holding onto the rocks. Her feet balancing on a tree limb. Crane Knelt down and pulled her up, feeling her freezing cold fingers against the warmth of his hands. "I guess fingerless gloves are good for some-things," she said looking him in the eyes.

"Be careful, it could still blow," Crane whispered watching the truck, which now looked very small. Lowri noticed that its holiday lights were flashing on and off. The gas was pouring out onto the snow like blood. Steam jetted out of the exhaust like dying breathes. Suddenly the police radio burst on – the Coca Cola Christmas jingle rolled out, distorted and slow. "Al – alwayyyyyssssss. . ."

Lowri staggered forward and looked at the picture of Father Christmas glugging a bottle of Cola, and thought she'd never touch the brand again. "It's dead. . . " Lowri stated.

"You mean *he's* dead honey," Crane said placing the blanket back around her shoulders. She saw the Truck slowly catch alight, a bright yellow flame tinted with blue and orange swept towards it.

"Yeah, ...right," Lowri muttered.

"Come on, back in the car. I'm gonna get you to that hotel in time for Christmas day." Lowri sat back inside the police vehicle and wondered if the search party would find Johnny or any of her friends. She doubted it. But there was always hope, after all, it was Christmas. There was always hope that she'd see them again. Always hope.

The End

Santa's Elite
By
Mark Cassell

Here amid the ranks of what are known as 'Santa's Little Helpers' we each have a story to tell. Most speak of their desire to make children smile (yeah, that old chestnut), for others it's the ability to construct presents parallel to those sold in stores (talent), and there are of course the guys involved with the alchemy behind Santa's magic (that stuff goes way over my head!). Everyone has an origins story, just like any superhero.

However, for some of us it's because Big Red is struggling with his workload. We're the Elite, Santa's Secret Service so secret all the other departments are oblivious to our year-round missions.

You see, 100 years ago Earth's population was around 2 billion, and now pushes 8. It grows by an estimated 74 million per year and sprints towards 10 billion – a total which scientists claim is the Earth's maximum capacity for resources as well as comfortable living. That's supposed to come about in only 30 or 40 years from now, so just think how Big Red must feel? That's a shit-tonne of work every Christmas Eve. His magic only stretches so far, you know.

The world is gonna get pretty damn

cramped if nothing's done about it.

That's where Santa's Elite comes in.

Before I get to the crack of it all and tell you what the Elite actually does, I should explain things from when I was a husband living in the UK with a wife who loved TV, chips, and chocolate, way more than she did me. I guess my catalyst was when France's Notre Dame cathedral burned. There was much more to it but while my ignorance at the time allowed me a short-sighted view, all I saw was that within 24 hours something like half a billion euros were pledged for restoration. No one died in that fire. Whereas back here in the UK, about 50 families remained unhoused from a tower block fire two years previous in which 64 people died.

We were one of those families.

When the fire ravaged our tower block, my wife and I were sitting in a shitty café down the street arguing about her infidelity... all the while my parents burned to death. Needless to say, the following two years were absolute hell. During which time she had another affair – the one of which I knew, at least. Please don't ask why I remained with her because I simply do not know. As pathetic as it is to say, I was scared to be alone and knew nothing and no one else.

When the Elite recruited me, my eyes were immediately opened. Wide. Trust me, it isn't climate change we have to worry about, it's the

Earth's doomed population. Up here in the North Pole it's still rigid with ice mountains – incidentally, I *love* my big duffle coat. But that's not my point.

The world is fucked, and the Elite are working all year round to save your arses. Well, those of you who've stayed off the Naughty List (yep, that really is a thing).

So, let's first talk about Christmas Eve of 2019, the day my life changed.

* * *

The kitchen was so small I had to shoulder closed the door, disconnecting myself from Kathy's domain just so I could open the oven. With the drone of the TV now a muffled Christmas tune of which I could never remember the name, the roar of the electric fan filled the room. Heat swept over me, but it smelled lovely.

We were still living in our temporary accommodation two years after our possessions became ash in the tower block fire.

"Kathy?" It was perhaps the first time I'd spoken all day. Wearing oven gloves that barely succeeded in their job, I placed the covered dish in the centre of our wobbly table. "Food's ready!"

I set out a pair of chipped plates on either

side of the dish and laid the mismatched cutlery. Just as I sat myself down, the door creaked open and my wife ambled into the room. Her familiar unwashed odour drifted towards me. Often it was from one extreme to the other, where she'd either reek of cheap perfume or stink of days' old sweat; there was never a pleasant in-between. She settled into the chair opposite, grunting. I removed the lid from the dish, allowing steam to billow as though the meal sighed. The meat and vegetables, the teasing heat, the aroma of those herbs I'd mixed with the gravy, was in fact pleasing.

Her voice shot across the table. "Not eating that."

She may as well have punched me.

As if to clarify, she added, "There's veg in it and everything."

I shrank.

There was more: "I'll eat the meat though."

I clenched my teeth to restrain the scream that clawed up my throat.

Keep your eyes down, I told myself, *keep them down, don't look up. Serve yourself, there's more for you if she doesn't want it.*

My fingers curled around the serving spoon.

Pressure from above, overhead and beyond that cramped kitchen as though our bed pressed through the bare floorboards, through the cracked ceiling and grimy light fitting. I wanted to hide beneath the table. To cry – but I never did. At least, never in front of this woman I shouldn't have married.

I inhaled the aroma as if it could blanket my deadened excitement – I was in fact annoyed at myself for even thinking she may enjoy the meal. Why did I occasionally bother to make something other than sausages, beans, and chips? Seriously, why? If it wasn't loaded with the ingredients for heart disease, diabetes, or cholesterol, she wasn't interested.

With the greatest of effort, I straightened up in my chair. The wood pressed awkwardly into my spine.

Kathy began chewing, loudly.

My efforts now washed away, it was like someone else's hand lifted the serving spoon to scoop the vegetables and meat. My plate, piled. Her plate, pathetic: just meat. I spied the green flecks of herbs and was surprised she didn't moan about that.

With a remarkably steady hand I picked up my fork, the one with a crooked prong. Then a knife (this one was at least straight). The sound of Kathy's wet mouthfuls drifted towards me, sliding across my skin to rake the back of my neck. My knife sliced through the meat, gravy oozing. Like mud. Using the knife, I pushed the vegetables up against the meat, and raised the loaded fork to my mouth.

In it went.

There was nothing wrong with it. It was pretty good, but... I glanced at Kathy. Her eyes were fixed on her meat-filled plate. Yeah, it looked like mud. A ruined meal, unappreciated. Why did I even bother cooking anything?

As it often was since hell's fire snatched away the pathetic life we had, only to make it even more pathetic, the meal was eaten in silence.

Mouthful after mouthful, Christmas Eve dragged on.

Eventually, Kathy's knife and fork clattered on the plate.

I looked up, waiting for her to leave the table, to shuffle off without a word and return to the lounge, to get back to whatever brain-numbing shit she'd been watching. A furrow creased her brow for a lightning second, and her lips parted as though to say something. She licked her lips, her tongue catching a herb that stuck to the corner of her mouth.

I lowered my gaze to my plate and continued the last few mouthfuls.

Her chair juddered on the linoleum floor and she grunted, then jerked upright. She stood, eyes rolling, and swayed as a strange silence filled the tiny kitchen. She dropped to her knees and her chin smacked the table edge. Her head snapped backwards. Plates and cutlery rattled.

And she sprawled across the floor.

I slowly got up from my chair, wiping my mouth with a sleeve.

The doorbell clanged, echoing from the lounge. Still to this day, I have no idea how I knew it was one of Santa's Little Helpers come to rescue me.

I simply *knew*.

Although the TV volume was cranked up, Mariah Carey singing about what she wanted for Christmas sounded muffled – I absolutely detest that tune. Every year it's everywhere! Don't even get me started on the fact that the other departments insist on playing the entire fucking album. Luckily, I don't often tread their offices; we Elite spend most of the time travelling around the globe.

When I pulled the front door until the chain went taut, cold air rushed in as a dishevelled face peered up through the gap. He had to be no more than 5-foot-tall, rugged with dark skin enough to suggest he was African. Red-rimmed eyes squinted beneath snow-flecked eyebrows and a floppy red and green hat (yes, we really do wear those things). Ice clumped his beard.

"Is she dead?" he asked.

I nodded. Again, it's something I simply

knew: Kathy was as dead as my love for her.

Without me touching it, the chain rattled and unhooked itself. I stepped back, suddenly feeling calm. Peaceful. And free.

I stepped aside to allow the man to enter the room. With both hands he held onto a rope over his shoulder, evidently dragging something on squeaky wheels. A thump and scrape echoed out in the hallway, and I guessed it bounced off a wall, adding another scuff to the council-neglected paintwork.

He wore faded shades of red and green, damp with snow and streaked with what looked like brick dust and flecks of rust. His scuffed boots flicked snow over the thread-bare carpet as he hauled behind him a Christmas parcel as large as a washing machine. It was a colourful box with uneven sides, crooked and dented, with crudely painted snowmen and Big Red – I suspected it had been painted by a child, or someone with absolutely zero artistic talent. The only thing that looked new, or at the very least in good condition, was the beautifully bound ribbon which was bunched up on what was presumably the lid. Such a pristine bow it almost shone in contrast to the dreary décor of our home.

At the time, I of course didn't know it was called a ribbon machine. A device the Elite simply refer to as the Machine. We each have our own, and it's up to us all to keep them in good working order. Our one and only tool of the trade, as it were.

I followed the man into the kitchen.

He released the frayed rope and crouched beside Kathy's lifeless body.

I felt nothing other than intrigue as he poked a finger into my wife's mouth, hooking out a soggy piece of ribbon the same red as the bow. He tucked it into his tunic pocket and stood.

"How are you feeling?" he asked, looking up at me. His eyes were as dark as his skin. Most of the snow had now melted and soaked his clothes, dripping onto the chipped linoleum.

I had no idea what to say.

He smiled with such perfect and very white teeth. "You good with this?"

I nodded.

"The name's Harold." His smile widened. "I know your name. It's good to meet you, Laurence."

Again, I nodded. I felt dumb.

"You're just going through the transition," he explained, "you'll be fine."

And he was correct. I was absolutely fine later, but right then I could only watch him do his thing.

We each have our own speciality. Harold's is choking, as demonstrated first hand to me when

I watched my wife die. And I must tell you about another fellow Elite member: Anne, whose speciality is the brain haemorrhage. She was once a neurosurgeon and although a rewarding job when people survived, she'd discovered a pleasure in the moment when people died. Santa's Elite recruited her in no time! Whereas I have a preference for the car crash. I sabotage the brakes on your vehicle by tying a piece of red ribbon somewhere under the bonnet (or *hood*, for you Americans – I cover most of the Western world, by the way). We're all both fast and invisible, so there's no hope in thinking you'd catch us in the act. That red ribbon, used by all of us here in the Elite, does its magic.

So, you understand, we pluck your name from Big Red's Naughty List and then we orchestrate the car crashes, the heart attacks, the classic fall-down-the-stairs-and-subsequent-neck-breaks. Oh, and of course the house fires…

But I'll get to those shortly.

Allow me to tell you that for those like my Kathy, and the many others on the various levels much, much worse than her, we Elite members put them into our Machines.

When I stood there in the kitchen and watched Harold untie the red bow on that curious box with its crude artwork, I had no idea what to expect. The smell of my failed meal and Kathy's body odour had now been replaced by a heavy, almost metallic odour.

The four sides clattered away. One slid across the linoleum and hit a cupboard door.

At first, I could not make out what the hell I was looking at. It was a peculiar contraption mostly of rusted panels bolted together. Rubber tubes and snaking cables connected various sections and linked a gaping cone at the top of the device. At the rear were three canisters fixed vertically beside one another: two were empty and reflected the kitchen lighting, while the other was filled with a sparkling mix of red and gold.

Very Christmassy, I thought.

Harold winked at me.

"Watch this," he said and lifted Kathy's body with impressive strength given his small stature and her considerable size, literally dead-lifting her overhead only to force her face-first into the cone.

I noted there were bloody smears around the edges.

Immediately the Machine hummed to life. The metal panels rattled as it devoured the body. Kathy's legs wobbled as though uselessly kicking. The floor shook, and the rumbling filled the room. Plates and glasses clinked somewhere in a cupboard, all the while the entire contraption rocked on its wheels.

Harold stepped away and came to stand at my side. From the corner of my eye I saw him look up at me. He was grinning.

The glass canisters began to fill with a purple liquid. By the time Kathy's feet vanished, both canisters were full.

Finally, the Machine quietened.

Harold approached the canisters and pressed a button. Something clicked, and a reel of brilliant red ribbon spun out to coil at his feet. With another prod of the button, the ribbon stopped.

"This will be yours," he told me and picked up the bunched ribbon. "It's traditional."

"What…" I licked my lips. "What do I do with it?"

"It's Big Red's little piece of magic, and you'll use it for a greater cause."

"I will?"

"Sure." He handed it to me.

The ribbon was warm.

And by the time I went for my induction as the newest member of Santa's Elite, that short reel of ribbon didn't last long. In fact, I soon used up both those canisters that were once my useless cheat of a wife.

* * *

I've been with the Elite for precisely a year, and unfortunately, I'm now up for a disciplinary. Or worse. A very rare case indeed because as long as we successfully continue to reduce the Earth's population growth, we're very much left to our own devices. Or indeed, *with* our own devices.

The thing is, I learned of a colleague who had a penchant for starting fires.

He was behind the tower block disaster, my old home where both my mother and father burned to death. This Elite member, a man named Monty, was usually more careful – before this, he had an excellent record. Instead of using his ribbon to sabotage only his target's 40-a-day habit of cigarette smoking, Monty managed to set fire to the whole apartment... which then became the entire building. As mentioned earlier, 64 people died.

When I found this out, I couldn't help myself and so confronted Monty.

We had a scuffle in the workshop, and what with my car-sabotaging ribbons and his fire-starting ribbons, we managed to start an electrical fire which destroyed the factory where they make presents.

Monty was crushed as the building collapsed (yay!), along with most of the guys in the workshop and adjacent offices (oops).

I suspect my disciplinary is going to be a harsh one and I really do want to keep my job, but at least I know I've done my bit for the planet. I've had an incredibly successful year, and I trust Big Red sees it that way and ultimately lets me off this minor hiccup. Given all my hard work alongside my colleagues in the Elite, I only hope it balances out the devastation here at the North Pole. Sure, the production line for present-building is majorly down – or perhaps temporarily halted – and the fatalities have been huge among our ranks, but the Elite have reduced the Earth's population by a considerable amount.

That should work in my favour, right?

If it hasn't balanced out, and I really have fucked it up for everyone this year, please accept my apologies.

The End

A Christmas Ghost Story, 1985
By
Amy Cross

"And that is what I saw as I was driven away from that wretched house," Mr. Robinson continued, as the light from a nearby candle danced across one side of his face. "A pale face, pressed against the window. Perhaps it is there still, awaiting my return. In which case, I can only promise that it shall be a very disappointed spirit indeed, for there is nothing in this world that could ever compel me to return... to Archington House!"

There was a pause, and then he rapped the top of his cane against the table – giving us all the signal that his story – the fourth of the night – had reached its terrifying conclusion.

"I say," Mr. Barnes said, leaning back in his creaking leather chair and dabbing at his brow with a handkerchief, "that was a rather unsettling tale, old chap."

Mr. Robinson smiled, clearly pleased with the reception of his story. He looked at Mr. Wellington, and then at myself, and his smile grew as he realized that he had made amends for his previous attempt. After all, while nobody had mentioned it, we were all keenly aware that last year Mr. Robinson had presented a rather poorly thought out story that scared absolutely no-one.

But that was 1894, and this is 1895, and the difference is quite striking.

"I must agree," I said, before reaching over and taking my glass of brandy from the table. "I'm not sure that I shall sleep well tonight." I glanced over at Ruthers, the waiter, and saw him standing nearby with a rather terrified expression on his face. "And you appear to have upset our dear Mr. Ruthers," I point out, as I nodded toward the poor fellow. "Look at him. He's quite aghast!"

"Not at all, Sir," Ruthers replied, shaking himself from his obvious state of shock. "I merely came to remind you that we shall be closing in ten minutes' time."

"Of course," Mr. Barnes said with a sigh. "I always forget that you close early on Christmas Eve. I should remember by now, though, should I not? After all, this is the tenth straight meeting of our annual Christmas club. Why, I'm not sure that Christmas would be Christmas without our little gathering of ghost stories."

"Something about Christmas seems to demand a good ghost story," Mr. Wellington mused, as we all turned and looked at the window. Snow was falling thick and fast now, blanketing the road outside the bar. "Perhaps it's the fault of the late Mr. Dickens. Some of his Christmas tales were decidedly ghoulish. Still, I have come to treasure this little tradition of ours. I trust, gentlemen, that we shall be here again this time next year, to regale one another with some more tales?"

He began to rise from his chair.

"Of course," Mr. Barnes said, "but wait! You have forgotten one thing!"

"Oh?" Mr. Wellington hesitated, his rump half risen from the plump cushions. "And what might that be?"

"It's not just the four of us tonight, is it?" Mr. Barnes continued. "You cannot have forgotten already that I brought a new addition to our little group." He turned and looked to his right, and we all followed his gaze. "Mr. Jackson," he added with a faint, anticipatory smile, "I trust that you have enjoyed yourself this evening. But I must insist that you grace us with a ghost story of your own. Such is, you must remember, the price of admission to our little group."

"I think Ruthers wants to lock up," Mr. Wellington suggested. "Isn't that right, Ruthers?"

"I can stay open for a little while longer," Ruthers replied, "if it suits the gentlemen."

We all kept our eyes on Mr. Jackson, who had hitherto remained quiet in his seat. At the start of the evening, this gentleman – who seemed rather shy and retiring – had placed himself at a short distance from our circle. In all honesty, the man seemed dreadfully unenthusiastic about our stories, and I had privately begun to wonder why he wanted to come at all. Now he seemed no more animated than before. Indeed, his face appeared rather thin and gaunt, more so than before.

"Well?" Mr. Barnes said with a smile. "Do you have a ghost story for us, Mr. Jackson?"

There was a pause, during which Mr. Jackson gave no indication that he had even heard the question, and then finally he shook his head.

"No," he said darkly, "I most certainly do not."

"No?" Mr. Barnes was still smiling, but I perceived that he was a little put out. "Come on, old chap, I explained how it works here. Every Christmas Eve we meet to tell one another ghost stories. If you want to join our little group, you simply must come up with a story of your own."

"Yes," Mr. Robinson added, "and you'd better make it a good one. We have standards, you know!"

Again, we waited, but again Mr. Jackson gave no indication that he was about to tell us a story. And then, just as I was beginning to think that I should prompt him, he got to his feet.

"I must bid you goodnight, gentlemen," he announced, "for I have a few miles to travel before I am home. I thank you must humbly for admitting me into your group for tonight. I have listened to your four ghost stories with interest, but I must say that I shall not be back next year. Nevertheless, I thank you again, and I hope that you continue to enjoy your little tradition."

With that, he turned to exit the club.

"Is that it?" Mr. Barnes asked. "Jackson, old man, I thought the whole idea was that you wanted to tell a ghost story? I mean, that's why you came, isn't it? To listen to our stories and to then tell us one of your own?"

"How can I," he replied as he stopped in the doorway and turned to us, "when they are all untrue?" There was a pause, as the fire continued to burn in the hearth. "Gentlemen," he continued finally, "I have no doubt that you enjoy yourselves here every Christmas Eve, telling your little stories. But they are lies, no matter how hard you each try to persuade one another that they are rooted in truth. These stories amuse you, and there is no shame in that, but they are mere fripperies. Therefore, you will I am sure understand if I take my leave."

He turned to walk away, but then – evidently seized by some fresh wave of anger – he turned back to us. For a moment, his face seemed contorted into a furious scowl.

"Gentlemen," he snapped, "I came here tonight because I thought you people might know something about ghosts! I thought I might learn! Instead I have listened to a series of pathetic little stories that would not even scare a dormouse! You have all clearly been making this all up as you go along. I cannot fathom how your minds can be so weak and credulous, but I assure you that I feel nothing right not other than pity and disgust. You are here for your entertainment, and for no other reason. You should all be ashamed of yourselves!"

Turning, he stepped out of sight before any of us could say a word.

Turning to the others, I saw that they all looked rather shocked.

"Well," Mr. Robinson said finally, "he's a barrel of laughs, isn't he?"

"I'm so dreadfully sorry," Mr. Barnes replied. "I never would have invited him if he hadn't seemed interested. I can't imagine why he came. After all, he knew full well the purpose of our little gathering."

"Some men are strange," Mr. Wellington said, and then he and his chair groaned in unison as he lifted his bulk from the cushions. "Why come to listen to ghost stories, when one does not believe in ghosts and does not even enjoy stories about them? Most peculiar, if you ask me. Anyway, Ruthers is obviously itching to close up, and I don't want to detain him for a moment longer. Let us not be Scrooges tonight, gentlemen. Let us be on our way. After all, we all have homes to go to, do we not?"

***

A short while later, having said my farewells to the others, I made my way toward to the hotel's foyer and began to contemplate my journey home. The bad weather had begun to really close in, but I felt that the walk might do me some good. I began to slip my hands into my gloves, but at that moment I reached the steps that led down into the foyer, and I realized that I could hear an angry, raised voice in the distance.

To my surprise, I saw that Mr. Jackson was remonstrating with a gentleman at the front desk.

"I want a carriage, damn it!" Mr. Jackson was shouting. "What is so difficult for you to understand? I want it here and I want it now!"

"Of course," the man stammered, "and one will be along shortly, I assure you. It's just that tonight is rather busy, and there aren't so many carriages on the streets tonight."

"I've had enough of your excuses," Mr. Jackson snapped. "I would remind you that I am an acquaintance of your employer. If I do not have a carriage within five minutes, I shall make sure that you lose your job!"

"Wait right here!" the terrified man said, as he turned and hurried toward the main door. "I'll have a carriage for you in just one moment!"

With that, he ran out into the snowy night, and Mr. Jackson turned and muttered something under his breath.

Still at the top of the steps, I realized that Mr. Jackson had not noticed my arrival. Indeed, he was still talking to himself as he made his way back across the foyer, and I watched as he approached the large mirror that hung at the far end. I felt rather uncomfortable, and I admit that I wanted nothing more than to hurry out without having to make conversation. At the same time, I knew that this would be impossible, and I began to realize that I would have to endure at least a brief exchange of pleasantries with the distinctly unpleasant Mr. Jackson.

I opened my mouth to call out to him.

"Stop it!" he gasped suddenly, as he leaned against the desk in front of the mirror. "Why can't you just leave me alone?"

I hesitated, wondering to whom he might be speaking.

"Just one night," he continued, sounding utterly exasperated. "That's all I ask. Can't you give me just one night of peace?"

I looked around, but there was certainly nobody else in the foyer, and indeed I knew that there could be nobody hidden away in another room. It seemed, then, that Mr. Jackson was talking to himself.

My discomfort was growing by the second.

"I know, I know," Mr. Jackson said after a moment, almost snarling as he stared into the mirror. "And I would, were I a braver man. Can't you be content with what you've already done to me? I should never have come out tonight. I had to listen to those fools and their idiotic stories. Did you hear their pathetic tales? Mark my words, not one of those men has ever seen a ghost. Not a real one."

Taking a deep breath, I began to worry that he would soon see me and think that I had been eavesdropping, so I hesitated a moment longer and then I cleared my throat.

Suddenly Mr. Jackson turned and glared at me with the angry intensity of a madman.

"I'm dreadfully sorry," I said, feeling rather as if I should explain myself. "I was only -"

"I'll have that fool's job!" Mr. Jackson snapped, before turning and storming toward the front door. "I shouldn't have to walk home! It's disgraceful!"

"Well," I muttered as he made his way out into the snow, "never mind."

For a moment, I wasn't quite sure what to do. There was a part of me that wanted to hurry after Mr. Jackson and explain myself more fully, but then I realized that the man's opinion was of no great concern. He seemed rather angry and disagreeable, and I fancied that I would likely never cross his path again. With that thought in mind, I resumed slipping my gloves onto my hands and I headed to the door myself, from where I made my way out onto the pavement and felt an immediate blast of cold air as snow drifted down from the night sky.

I glanced along the street and saw Mr. Jackson furiously walking away, and then – to my surprise – I noticed that while he was walking alone, his reflection had a companion.

Mr. Jackson was making his way past a shop, and in the shop's window there was not only his reflection but also the reflection of a young woman wearing a white dress. She seemed to be talking to Mr. Jackson, and he to her, yet this woman appeared only as a reflection. On the actual pavement, there was no sign of her.

I told myself that this was merely an illusion, that the girl must be inside the shop, but at that moment Mr. Jackson moved past a completely different building, a restaurant, and I saw that his reflection was still being pursued by the strange woman. It was as if he walked with a companion who was visible only in the glass.

Suddenly he turned and shouted at the woman, and then he resumed walking. She went with him, keeping pace and seemingly arguing with him.

Hearing the door opening nearby, I saw Ruthers coming out from the foyer.

"I'm terribly sorry, Sir," he said, clearly a little startled, "would you like me to find a carriage for you?"

"No, I'm alright, thank you," I replied. "One of your colleagues has already found it rather difficult to arrange for carriages tonight. It is Christmas Eve, after all."

"I shall see you next year, then," Ruther replied. "Assuming we are to be graced again with your annual gathering?"

"Of course," I told him. "Christmas wouldn't be Christmas without some ghost stories."

"And..." He hesitated, and suddenly he seemed rather troubled. "And will Mr. Jackson be joining you from now on?" he asked finally.

"I rather think not," I said, and I saw the relief in the man's expression. "He did not seem to enjoy our ghost stories at all."

"I dare say he didn't," Ruther replied, "not after what happened to his daughter."

He turned to go back inside.

"His daughter?" I said cautiously. "I'm afraid I do not know the gentleman at all, and I certainly have no knowledge of his circumstances."

"It was most dreadful," Ruther said, stopping in the open doorway. "I believe it occurred about five years ago. Mr. Jackson lived with his daughter, just the two of them alone. She was a troubled young woman, and they said that eventually one morning he found her hanging from the rafters in her bedroom. It was the morning she was due to be married. She had left a note in which she blamed him for all her unhappiness. I know a man who lived near them, and he said the arguments would rage all night. All the neighbors heard them. Until she died, that is." He hesitated. "Some say they still hear them," he added finally, "even after she died."

"Indeed," I replied, "and that -"

Suddenly I thought of the strange woman who had seemed to be following Mr. Jackson, and who appeared only in reflection. The more I remembered her, the more I began to realize that, indeed, she had seemed to be wearing a white dress that could have been intended for a wedding.

"Are you quite alright, Sir?" Ruther said. "You look like you've seen a ghost."

"I'm fine," I told him, although I felt rather flustered. "Now, if you'll excuse me, I must begin my walk home. I should like to get back before midnight, to see my wife and children before Christmas Day begins."

Once Ruther had gone back inside, I began to set off, although after a moment I stopped and looked back the other way. Mr. Jackson was long since out of view, of course, but for a few seconds I thought of him out there somewhere, still arguing out loud as he walked. I thought, too, of the mysterious girl who could only be seen by her reflection, and I caught myself wondering whether she could possibly be the poor dead daughter. If that were the case, though, why would Mr. Jackson have attended our annual Christmas ghost story club? And why had he not told us about the strange creature that seemed to pursue him through the streets?

I turned, feeling a momentary chill.

And then some children began to sing nearby, and I saw them standing happily around a makeshift fire. I walked toward them and put a penny in their hat, which caused them to sing louder still, and as I walked away, I felt filled with the spirit of festive cheer. I was already looking forward to the following year's Christmas ghost stories, and I knew I would have to really come up with something ghastly in order to entertain the others. There was plenty of time, though, and I would certainly tackle the job with great enjoyment and gusto.

After all, what kind of man would not enjoy a ghost story at Christmas?

The End

The Christmas Miracle
By
Chris Miller

Womp-wump…womp-wump…womp-wu—

"Oh, my God…" Stanley whispered to himself as his shuddering hands gripped the steering wheel. His breathing was harsh, but slow, his exhales still making barely discernable clouds in front of his face while the old car did its best to warm up as the cold pressed in all around it.

The street was barren before him, little more visible than the thick clods of snow battering the windshield. Sound was likewise scant. The only thing he could hear were the sharp inhales of his breaths and the incessant drone of the wipers diligently pushing the snow aside.

Womp-wump…womp-wump…womp-wump.

The deserted, wintery landscape before him suddenly chilled his blood. It wasn't the cold itself, but rather the sight of the normally busy street sporting nothing but the piling snow and his rumbling old car. The lack of sounds added a layer to his chill that now settled into his bones. No beeping horns, no people chattering into cell phones, no cars crunching over the snow.

There was nothing. Only the rumble of his engine, the purr of the exhaust, the *womp-wump* of the wipers as they—

The body next to him shifted in the seat and slumped against the door. Stanley nearly barked a scream as the sound of the corpse's cheek dragging down the window shrieked in the cabin of the car like nails over a chalkboard. His hands never moved from their death grip on the wheel, but his neck craned around ninety degrees, his eyes wide and horrified over his gaping mouth as the body slumped unnaturally in the seat against the door. When she stopped moving, Stanley just gaped at her, his lips quivering. What had he done? What was he *doing?* If someone came along and saw her face pressed comically against the window, probably with glazed and dead eyes open and mouth and nostrils pulled wide against the glass, he would be finished. He wouldn't have a chance.

And he couldn't let that happen. Not yet.

He dropped the car into drive with tremulous hands and pulled forward, crunching over the ice and snow packed beneath his tires, she slumped back against the seat, hiding her face from sight for the moment. That was good. Anything that gave him some time was welcomed now. Jamie needed the time. Cammie was with him at the hospital now, watching him fade. He knew he should be there with their son as his life drained with his failing heart.

But instead, he was here. With *her.*

136

He glanced sidelong at her as the car rolled over a significant swatch of hard-packed snow. Her head lolled back and forth, the face still looking away from him, pressed into the side pillar of the car by the window. Then she was mostly still as the car's ride smoothed.

He sighed, looking back to the empty road, streetlamps seeming to glow bright and fade into obscurity as he approached and passed them on either side of the car. His mind raced, nearing panic. What would he do when he got back to the hospital? How would he make sure they did what he needed them to do with her body? To save his boy?

He and Cammie had been as patient as could be expected when Jamie had been put on the transplant list. Children were moved up high on the list, but it didn't mean there would be an eligible donor in time. There were a *lot* of kids who needed transplants, and there were only so many donors at the right time and place—and with the right blood type—to give those on the list a chance. Jamie had seemed to take it about as well as one could hope for. But that was to be expected. All he could really understand was he was sick. Only seven years old. So sweet, so beautiful, so full of...

Well, not full of life. Not if he didn't get a donor, and soon. And now, with his vitals hardly keeping him alive and Cammie becoming more and more desperate, they were out of time. The doctor had asked them if they were praying folks, to which they had both nodded. Cammie was. She never missed Mass if she could avoid it, and her prayer life was as persistent as an angry gnat. Stanley was another story. He joined his wife at Mass when it was convenient, did his obligatory once per year confession that he hardly more than mumbled his way through with a list of sins he may or may not have committed. It was just routine. Something he did because it was important to Cammie. Because it was important to her that they raise their boy in the faith.

But he really *wasn't* a praying man. Hadn't been for many years now, and while there was a short-lived resurgence when they'd received Jamie's diagnoses, it had faded along with his hopes of seeing his son healthy and whole again, living his best life with far more years ahead of him than Stanley or Cammie would have. He'd been unable to continue to ask an indifferent deity for help with his dying son. There would be no donor for his boy. Not in time. And what better time of year for it to happen than on Christmas Eve.

"He may pull through until morning," the doctor had told them earlier that evening. "There's always hope, but I'm...I'm not optimistic. I'm so sorry."

"A donor," Cammie had muttered, not really a question *or* a statement. Just words. Words of hope. Of dread.

Of desperation.

The doctor had smiled sympathetically, a look that nearly sent Stanley into a rage of violence right then and there, despite its genuineness. Doctors, with their tack-on empathy that, no matter how unfeigned, they were able to toss into a bag and forget about as soon as they were out of sight of the family of their suffering and dying patients.

There would be no donor. They were sitting on their hands, watching their son die. He couldn't let that happen. He couldn't do *nothing*. His boy deserved better than that.

The droning crunch of the snow beneath his tires and the *womp-wump* of the wipers had a hypnotic effect. Despite the tension in his arms and shoulders and head, he could feel his eyes growing heavy. He was exhausted. The last time he'd slept was a total mystery to him. And now the rush that had filled his body when he'd put the .22 to the side of her head and pulled the trigger was flushing out of his system, leaving him drained.

He decided he needed music. Something to drown out the snow and the wipers and the—

What the hell is that sound? he thought as his ear tingled and he turned to look at her.

She was slumping more in the seat now, her shoulders rubbing against the leather and making farting sounds as she slinked deeper into the seat and further out of sight from any prying eyes. He decided it was a good thing, but the sight of her open and glazed eyes sent fresh shivers through him as clouds of breath blew from his mouth faster and faster.

He slapped the radio's knob and the car filled with the brash assault of static. Strange, winding sounds seemed to snake through the white noise, and he began to fumble with the frequency knob to find a station. Anything was better than hearing the wipers and the snow and the dead woman next to him farting over the seat.

For several moments, there was nothing. He went all the way to the end of the frequencies with nothing more than static along the way. His eyes squinted at this. He should have found *something* on the dial. In town he usually could pick up more than half a dozen stations with crystal clarity and another fifteen or more with some haze. But there was nothing. Not a chime, not a twang, not a voice.

He turned back the other way.

As he passed where the dial had been set when he started and began traversing the stations to the other direction, the static continued. It made no variation at all as the needle crept further and further to the left and Stanley's frustration began to grow.

Just before reaching the opposite extreme of the frequencies, a station came on in perfect, crystalline clarity, and he stopped turning the knob. A jingle began to play, a warm guitar riff that typically sent shivers of joy through his body, but now seemed nearly obscene in the cab of his car. His passenger seemed not to mind as she slumped further still in the seat, her legs and butt now fully in the footwell, her head cocked at an odd angle on the back of the seat. He caught a glimpse of the small bullet hole in her temple, which sported the smallest trickle of now-drying blood. There was no exit wound. The small round had never come out. And that was fine. He didn't need her brain. *Jamie* didn't need her brain. What they needed was packed neatly and wholly undisturbed beneath her breast.

"Jingle bell, jingle bell, jingle bell rock..." the radio squawked, the tittering guitar licks shrill in the old sound system.

Another rise of snow put the car into a rocking shudder, and his passenger's mouth opened and clacked shut three times. To his disgust and horror, it had seemed perfectly in time with the music on the radio, as if his fresh victim were singing along to the happy tune. It was an obscene sight. The eyes never blinked and her slumped form with the head cocked so unnaturally and with the small hole in her temple with the weeping tear of blood seemed to mock him.

He hit the knob again and the radio fell silent. Her corpse didn't seem to get the message, however. She continued to bounce and bob as the car rumbled on, teeth clacking together in time to music that only she seemed able to hear now.

It's all for you, Jamie, he thought as tears stung his eyes and dread filled his bowels like bricks. *You're going to live your life. We needed a Christmas miracle, but God ain't listening. I hope you remember that in the coming years, Jamie. You have to take life by the horns and* make *your own miracles. No one else will do it for you.*

As if in agreement with his thoughts, the corpse nodded sharply as it folded into the footwell fully now, the head thumping against the glove box. She was propped now, staring at him with lifeless eyes, the weeping temple a macabre wink to the absurdity of it all.

He brought his eyes back to the snowy road before him, the oddly *empty* street that might have seemed serene under different circumstances, the yellow glow of the sodium vapor streetlamps casting a pleasant sheen over the landscape before him. He wasn't far from the hospital. Only a mile or so. Stanley had no idea what he would do when he got there. How would he get her inside for the transplant his son so desperately needed?

No answer was forthcoming. He hadn't planned any of this out. In the previous weeks, he had considered committing suicide. He was a donor himself, and being his son's biological father, he would be a good candidate for the transplant. But he'd been too cowardly or too selfish to go through with it. He thought he'd perhaps been both of those things. He wanted his

142

son to live more than anything. But he also wanted to *see* his son live. Wanted to be there to see him grow up, go to school, meet someone and get married. Maybe even make him a grandfather.

With what he'd done now, tonight, even that would be taken from him. Mostly, anyway. He knew he was headed to prison. Possibly even death row if whatever lawyer he managed to land wasn't crafty. But he thought he could manage a life in prison sentence, given the circumstances. He was a grieving and scared father acting in desperation, not malice. It hadn't been premeditated. He hadn't stalked this poor woman. Hadn't sought her out for murder. It just happened. Something she had said—

"That makes it okay, Stanley?"

The voice startled him so much that he jerked the wheel. Beneath the thick layering of snow was packed ice, and the car slid completely into the opposing lane and fishtailed before he was able to get it under control. He'd stopped breathing at some point, and when it returned it was in barks of exasperation as his adrenaline receded and his fingertips began to tingle.

That had been close. But never mind how close it had been, who had spoken?

Though he knew he was alone in the car with the corpse, he glanced first into the rearview mirror and then over his shoulder into the back seat. Empty. Nothing there but an old blanket and an ancient Snickers wrapper in the floorboard.

He brought his eyes back to the road. They were wide now, and though his breathing was getting back to something close to even, it was deep and harsh. Pinpricks of electricity began needling him at the base of his skull and down his back. He'd heard it, right? The voice? It hadn't been in his head. It had been audible. Right there with him.

But he was alone. Aside from the crunching snow and the *womp-wump* of the wiper blades, there was no sound. He felt that electric tingle spread from his shoulders and down to his elbows. Could feel that sinking, lead brick in his gut dropping lower still, as though it were reaching for his knees.

You're losing it, he thought. *Your mind is all out of sorts. You've murdered a woman. The reason doesn't matter, you're a MURDERER! And now you're hearing voices.*

The snowy road stretched out before him in the bleak cold.

He decided he should try the radio again. Anything was better than stewing in his grief and guilt and desperation. Something to kill the voices now coming to him from...*from where?*

His hand dropped from the wheel and was heading for the knob on the radio. Only, before he'd reached halfway to the stereo, the lights on the dial suddenly came to life and *Jingle Bell Rock* came back on, loud and tinny, blaring into his ears with its delightful riff and joyful voices.

He cried out, his hand jerking away from the knob involuntarily and clasping over his mouth to silence his outburst. He began to gasp, and his breathing once more came in uneven hitches as his wide eyes lingered a moment too long on the glowing dial.

When the car began to swerve beneath him again, he grasped the wheel in both hands, struggling to regain control. He wasn't going fast, but the car had slung nearly sideways twice before he managed to straighten it. His nerves were fried and his whole body began trembling. Stanley decided he needed a few moments before going on to the hospital where he hoped his son would be saved and he would be taken into custody.

He pulled the car to the curb and it slid to a stop over the snow. He threw the shifter into park and laid his head on the steering wheel, where he began to weep, quietly at first, then growing in volume and ferocity until he was wailing in full-on sobs.

"Jingle bell, jingle bell, jingle be—" the radio mocked his grief and he angrily slapped the knob on the stereo. It went quiet and dark once more, leaving him with only the monotonous drone of the wipers as he shivered and cried.

"I asked you a question," the voice from before spoke again, causing Stanley's head to jerk

up from the wheel as he swatted tears from his face and turned. His breath caught in a gasp, sure that he would see the woman's corpse crawling up from the footwell next to him, dead eyes staring dully at him, the mouth peeling open in a snarl.

But she neither spoke nor crawled, though the eyes did seem to bore into him, not letting him free. Stanley gulped loudly, his throat clicking dryly, and he squinted his teary eyes. He'd heard the voice. It was as audible as the *womp-wump* of the wipers. As audible as the radio had been with its blaring, jolly tune. Yet it was only he and the corpse, who showed no evidence of speaking now, no evidence of life at all.

Still, he spoke to it.

"Did you…" he began and trailed off, gulping once more with a concerted effort. "You couldn't have—"

"What did you expect, Stanley?" the still, unmoving corpse asked him. The dead eyes never moved. The pale lips never formed a shape. But it was her. He knew it like he knew he loved his son. Like he knew he would do *anything* for his baby boy. The one dying even now in a sterile room at the hospital another mile up the street.

She *had* spoken to him. Asked him the terrible question. The one that had no real answer, no real purpose other than torment.

His trembling hand covered his quivering lips in an expression of horror. Was he going mad?

146

Was his mind tearing itself apart because of what he'd done to this woman in an act of parental desperation? It couldn't be real. She didn't move. Didn't breathe. Even the trickle of blood from her temple was still now, drying and crusting to her skin. But it was *her*. Speaking to him from beyond.

"After all I've done for your boy," she began again, unmoving, *"you do this to me? Do you really think this is going to save your boy? And is it worth it? Damning your soul that your son might live?"*

Stanley wasn't breathing. His eyes seemed unable to blink. His hand was clutching his face now, not merely coving his mouth, but digging into the skin as though preparing to tear it from his face.

With an effort, he pulled his hand away and rested it upon his chest, breathing deeply in an effort to control his now galloping heart, threatening to tear free of his chest and vanish into the night.

"I told you there was still hope. There's always hope so long as there's breath in Jamie's body. But this..."

A sudden squawk caused him to nearly leap out of his skin. He cried out a soft gasp, jerking his head around every which way, looking for the source of the sound. He saw nothing in front of him down the street, only the snow and the lights and the distant neon sign of the ER a less than a mile ahead. The sidewalks were deserted, and everything seemed to be sleeping or dead.

It wasn't until he looked back to her corpse that he noticed the red and blue colors glowing and fading and glowing on her pale skin. Still, his mind couldn't process what it was taking in. His mouth moved, his eyes narrowed and widened, but he could form no words. As he did this, the corpse remained still, perfectly quiet, perfectly dead, holding the precious miracle within her chest. Only...

Was she smiling?

He blinked several times, gazing upon the pale skin with the glowing and fading hues and... she *was* smiling. God help him, *the corpse was smiling at him!*

"What do you think he'll have to say about this, Stanley?" the mocking corpse said to him with unmoving lips. *"You think he'll give you a pass because your precious little boy is dying in his bed up the street?"*

He heard a car door slam shut somewhere outside and his eyes jerked to the rearview mirror even as the corpse began to laugh at him in a mocking cackle full of pitiless mirth. As the cackles rose in volume and spite, a cold blanket enveloped Stanley as he saw the policeman approaching from the car behind him, a silhouette in the flashing lights.

"Oh, my dear God!" he whispered as his hand moved independently of his will and clutched his wife's .22 revolver inside his jacket pocket.

"What are you going to do now?" the wretched thing asked him. *"What will you tell him? Are you going to tell him what happened? What you've done?"*

The laughter rose again in haunting wails, welding his vertebrae into a frozen, iron rod. His breath caught as the policeman drew closer, and Stanley's hand pulled free of his jacket, white knuckles wrapped around the grip of the small gun.

"Why don't you tell him you just need a Christmas miracle?"

Then a hand was rapping on his window.

#

Earlier, Stanley had been sitting next to his son's bed, holding his little hand in both of his. Stanley felt empty as he watched his boy wither away. All around the room were vases of flowers and balloons and little stuffed animals. Hearts and notes of well-wishes and love adorned them all. In the corner of the room was a small table upon which stood a short Christmas tree. It stood less than three feet tall and was adorned in garlands of silver and blue, ornamental balls hanging from its branches. Beneath it were a few wrapped presents, things they hoped to open with Jamie in the morning, which by all estimations, would be his son's last Christmas, if he made it through the night at all.

"Mr. Denton?" a soft, sympathetic voice drifted to him.

He rose his head from its bowed position and blinked several times as his eyes rested on Dr. Sheila Mead. She stood in the entrance to the room, her white coat draped over a denim blouse open at the collar and black slacks. Her blond hair was pulled back in a loose ponytail, and her tired face bore compassion despite her obvious exhaustion.

He smiled weakly at her and nodded. "Doctor."

She returned his smile, as weak as his own.

"Still sleeping?"

Stanley sighed and glanced at Jamie.

"All night."

"That's to be expected," she said.

The statement hung in the air like a toxic cloud, and it threatened to break Stanley's heart into even smaller pieces. He choked back a fresh swell of tears and struggled to say something, *anything*, to take the focus off the tragedy he was facing.

"M-my wife," he said and coughed as he fought down the urge to cry. "My wife should be back—"

"She just got in," Dr. Mead inserted. "She's on her way up."

"That's good," Stanley nodded. "She's so tired, she needed some rest."

"Yes," she said. "I think you could use a break yourself."

Stanley shook his head.

"I don't want to leave him. I want to be here if...if he..."

This time he could not control the tears and they sheeted his face in warm rivers. The doctor crossed the room as he hid his face in his hands. She placed a comforting one of her own upon his shoulder and squeezed.

"He's stable for now, Mr. Denton," she said. "He's sleeping and he's comfortable. Your wife is back, and she can sit with him. Why don't we go grab a cup of coffee?"

He began to protest, thinking of his boy, his condition, the holiday upon them that would likely be stripped of all joy for the rest of their lives, but the doctor was adamant.

"Mr. Denton, I—"

"Stanley, please," he said and almost laughed. "You're damn near family at this point, doc."

"Very well, Stanley," she said. "And call me Sheila."

He looked up to her and patted the top of her hand, smiling.

"Sheila."

"Come on," she said. "It's my treat. You need to get out and stretch your legs. I know a great place down the street. Best coffee in town."

It took his wife joining in when she arrived to convince him to go get a cup of coffee with the doctor and get his bearings. Finally, he relented.

They had shared a slice of pecan pie as they had their coffee, and the doctor had tried to give him hope.

"The donor list is...well, it is what it is, I guess. So many people in need of transplants, all of them precious to someone. There are fathers and mothers and grandparents and—"

"And children," he cut her off bitterly.

Her face flushed and she gripped her coffee in both hands, nodding.

"And children, yes," she said with a sigh. "Look, I know there's nothing I can say that will ease your grief, but I wanted to encourage you if I'm able. I won't get your hopes up, I don't think that's fair. The chances of a matching donor coming in tonight, or even in the next few days, is very slim. But there's still hope, Stanley. So long as there's breath in Jamie's body, there's hope."

His eyes ached from the tears. His jaw was set and locked, his teeth grinding. He wanted to *do* something. He *needed* to do something. He was Jamie's father, goddamnit, and a father was supposed to protect his children. Since the diagnoses, he'd never felt more helpless.

"Hell," she went on with a smirk, "B-negative is rare, but I've seen it happen before. In fact, if we had an O-negative heart come in we could move forward. That's the universal donor."

Stanley glanced up at her, eyes rimmed red.

"Universal?"

She nodded. "That's right. Persons with O-negative blood type are considered the universal donor. AB-positive is the universal recipient, and it just so happens that's Jamie's blood type. So, there's hope."

Stanley's face contorted with something he couldn't define. It was grief, but it was also something else. Something he'd come to believe was worse than grief, something he'd until this moment sworn off as a merciless monster.

Hope.

Doctor Mead took a deep breath, finished her coffee, and sighed as she set it down.

"Maybe we'll even get lucky," she said with the mildest of laughs. "We could have an accident on the way back to the hospital. You're his father and I happen to be O-negative myself. We're both donors."

Stanley gazed at her, his eyes narrowed, but not with confusion. He could see she had taken his reaction as being hurt, and she began to apologize.

"No, no," he said, waving her off. "I-I just...I don't know what I'm feeling. I just wish there was something I could *do*."

He felt a pang of guilt when she smiled and placed a hand on his, giving it a reassuring squeeze. But he shoved the feeling aside.

"I understand," she said, her voice an ocean of comfort. "We'll keep praying for a Christmas miracle. This is the time of year *for* miracles, as they say. Don't lose hope."

He smiled back to her through wet eyes, thinking of his wife's revolver in the car.

#

The policeman rapped on the window a second time as Stanley replayed reaching past the doctor, snatching the small revolver from the glove box. The way her head bucked slightly even as her confused eyes began to shine with realization as he'd fired. The way she mocked him with phantom laughter and a leering grin he was sure could not be there.

The revolver was in his lap when he turned to face the cop, a flashlight now beaming, nearly blinding him. His heart was tearing through his chest and up through his throat. In another moment it would splatter to his lap, angry and quivering.

He heard the cop gasp.

The cone of light had shifted from Stanley's eyes and fell upon the corpse of Dr. Sheila Mead beside him and the crunch of snow sounded under shuffling feet as the cop spoke.

"Jesus!" the cop gasped, his hand going for his sidearm. "Keep your hands where I can see them! Step away from the—"

But Stanley's hand was dropping the transmission back into drive. The tires spun over the ice and snow, but the car began moving. There were more barking orders from the cop, but to Stanley's surprise, no shots came. The engine was revving, and the car was sliding back onto the street, the flashing lights of the police cruiser growing smaller.

He continued to gain speed, racing to the hospital. He hadn't had a plan before, and he didn't have much of one now. All he could think to do was to get to the hospital and scream at whomever he saw first to get Dr. Mead inside and put her heart inside his son's chest. They would take him then, take him away for the rest of his life. But maybe, if God was listening to his desperate pleas for that fabled Christmas miracle, it might work.

The policeman was in pursuit now, siren wailing behind them, but Stanley didn't falter. He powered forward, pressing the accelerator further and further down to the floor, both hands on the wheel now, his left still clutching the revolver. Sweat broke out on his brow despite the chill. His heart raced. His limbs tingled. His stomach rolled.

"The final stretch, eh?" Dr. Mead laughed at him as he raced. *"The flight of the damned! Don't waver now, Stanley! You're so fucking close!"*

"Shut up!" he screamed and glanced at the corpse whose body shook with the car, her head bobbing up and down like a terrible parody of a bobble-head doll.

"Maybe they'll save your boy after all," she mocked in a loud, hissing whisper. *"Wouldn't that be wonderful? Maybe they'll save your boy and bring a little JOY to the world!"*

As her maniacal laughter boomed beside him, the radio suddenly sparked back to life, the lights rising to their shine and the music coming back in a warbling arc until it was to full volume once more.

"That's the jingle bell! That's the jingle bell! That's the jingle bell roooooooocccckkkkkk!"

Stanley screamed, jolting in horror, and jerked on the wheel. The car began to slide, the red and blue flashes once more growing larger in his mirror, the shriek of the siren blaring all around him. The dead doctor's corpse continued its cackle of cruel laughter as the neon sign of the Emergency Room filled his vision.

He jerked the wheel a final time, but it was too late. The car veered back to the left and began to slide toward a large concrete pillar, which filled the passenger window in its entirety. The corpse cackled a final time before the impact, driving home its mocking torment.

"The hospital!" it howled. *"It's a Christmas miracle!"*

A half-second later, the sounds of exploding glass and crunching metal erupted all around him, and his face was met with a giant, white pillow. It didn't feel like a pillow, more like a sack of dried corn hitting him across the face. He felt a barely warm stickiness spatter the right side of his face and there were terrible ripping sounds as something was eviscerated next to him.

Then all was still. He pulled his face from the now deflating airbag, noticing the droplets of crimson on it and his sleeve. His mind was reeling, but this sight focused his thoughts and brought his dread to a fever-pitch.

He cried out when he saw her. The side of the car had caved in all around her, and part of the engine from the passenger side was visible in the seat. What little was left of Dr. Mead looked like a bomb had exploded inside hamburger meat. She was torn apart. He found her head in the back seat, still glaring at him with dead eyes and the hint of a sneer on the blood coated lips. But that wasn't the worst part. It wasn't the part that caused all hope to flee from him like the merciless beast it was, carrying his efforts and prayers into an abyss of indifferent mockery.

The engine had torn through her chest. Little more than pulp was left, any hopes of her heart going into his son gone.

"No!" he gasped as he fumbled for the door handle.

As the door howled on bent hinges, Stanley Denton rose, stumbling into the freezing night. Medical staff were rushing towards him, and the wailing police car skidded to a stop behind him. The siren barked a final time and then stopped, but the flashing lights remained.

His ears were ringing as he looked about the scene before him, at his ruined and blood-soaked car. Tears blurred his vision as sobs burst from him in agonizing moans of despair and shame and helplessness. He couldn't save his son.

There was *nothing* he could do for his sweet, little boy. Jamie would die. His prayers had gone unanswered. There would be no miracle for his family this Christmas Eve.

"Show me your hands!" the cop cried somewhere behind him, but Stanley hardly noticed. He was watching the medical staff, backing away now as the cop barked orders. Stanley scanned their faces, recognizing some, others unfamiliar to him. He'd come to know so many of them since the diagnoses, in all the time he and his wife and boy had spent at this place while his son died more and more every day.

"My son needs a miracle!" Stanley screamed, but not to any of the onlookers. It was to God. To the universe. To *anyone* or *anything* that might listen.

"I'm not gonna say it again, asshole!" the cop screamed, his voice cracking with tension. "Show me your fucking hands!"

Stanley looked to his hand, the one holding the revolver. He was seconds away from a lifetime in jail, or being killed in the street by a frightened cop. But instead of dropping the gun, he smiled beneath teary eyes, thinking of something Dr. Mead had said.

"We could have an accident on the way back to the hospital. You're his father and I happen to be O-negative myself. We're both donors."

He was Jamie's father. *He* was a donor. His

not-really-a-plan-at-all to use the doctor's heart for his son had failed, but maybe God had heard his cries after all. Maybe.

But not if the cop blasted him full of holes first.

Stanley dropped to his knees, weeping openly, and caught sight of his wife. She was in the doorway, screaming something he couldn't hear, being held back by a large security officer. Tears streaked her face and makeup ran in streaks over her confused face.

He smiled at her.

"Make sure he gets it, baby!" he yelled to her over the din of the screaming cop and the gasps of the onlookers. "And tell him he's always had my heart!"

She heard him. The horror in her eyes was absolute. Her mouth fell open and he thought she might collapse. He couldn't see that. Couldn't watch the love of his life collapse under the weight. She was on the cusp of losing her son and now about to watch her husband ripped from her to jail or the grave only hours or days before her boy would be gone forever. But she'd been praying too. Praying for a miracle.

Stanley lowered his head and sighed a final prayer.

"God," he whimpered as he brought the barrel up to his face and the cries of the cop began to transform into shrieking screams. "My boy needs a miracle. Give him one, would ya?"

Stanley tasted the cold metal in his mouth a second before his head bucked back. The world began to darken as he tumbled to the snow, hoping the cop wouldn't open fire on him and destroy the part of him a child needs from a parent more than anything else in the world.

Their heart.

No shots came, and as his body settled into the snow, he thought he could hear that song playing somewhere in the distance. The one so full of joy. The one that used to make he and his wife begin dancing every time they heard it.

"What a bright time, it's the right time to rock the night away..."

As the blood pooled around his head, stark in the still falling snow, Stanley Denton died, hoping for a Christmas miracle.

The End

Down the Bizarro Watering Hole
By
Kevin J. Kennedy

On the last work day of the year, the minutes seemed to pass by slower than any other day. Tiffany could never understand why they had to work on Christmas Eve anyway. No one did anything. The entire morning was spent killing time. They always got a half day though there was no set time to leave. The entire staff had to sit around waiting on an email coming from the owner, telling them they could all go home. It could be anytime between twelve- thirty and two-thirty. Most of the staff took turns sneaking out to buy last minute Christmas gifts. Since Tiffany already had in what she needed she would spend the entire day surfing the net. The Christmas party had been the night before and she was still hungover—another reason that it made no sense to have anyone in on the twenty fourth. It was just all-round stupid.

At ten past two the email arrived. By this point Tiffany was at a boiling point. She had popped out at lunch time and had two double vodka cokes to take the edge off but returning to work to sit and wait on a stupid email had put her in a foul mood. She had no plans for Christmas Day as her family all lived across the sea and her presents had been posted already, so she had nothing in particular to do, which suited her fine. When the email popped into her inbox, she pushed the power button on her PC and shouted, "Have a good Christmas everyone!" as she walked out the door. She could not be bothered with all the kisses and cuddles and fake platitudes. While there was no one in the office that she particularly disliked, there was also no one she particularly liked either. It was a job. She was there to make money to pay her bills and that was all.

Tiffany's friends were all spending Christmas Day with their families and none of them planned to get drunk on Christmas Eve. They all wanted to be fresh for the day and enjoy Christmas dinner, which she could understand. A few of them had invited her to join them at their family dinners and while she knew the offers were genuine, she didn't want to be the hanger-on at another family's special day. She was quite content to spend time alone, never being one to feel sad about things like that. Christmas was a special day when you were with the ones you loved, but when you were on your own, it was just another day. There was no sadness attached. It was just a fact.

As Tiffany stepped out of the elevator and made her way out of the building, she decided that another few drinks would bring her back to the land of the living, then she would head home and find a few good movies to watch while having a last few drinks in her apartment. She planned to have a very long lie- in the morning. That would be her Christmas gift to herself.

Walking along the street she decided to head towards her apartment and find a bar close to home, so she could get back quickly and get into her jammies. She had bought new PJs for the night, a tradition that she had never let go of, even though she was all alone. They had little cartoon reindeers on them that wore Santa hats. She had changed her bed covers before going to the Christmas party the day before and had slept on the sofa last night for the few hours' sleep she got, so the bed would be fresh and inviting when she got in. She was looking forward to chilling out and was running through movies she may watch in her mind when she noticed a new bar across the street. The red neon sign read 'Bizarro,' and she thought it seemed like a strange name for a bar but decided it would do for a quick few drinks and crossed the road.

Inside, the bar was almost empty. She felt quite happy with that, feeling no need for Christmas revellers bothering her and making small talk. She perched herself on a bar stool with some difficulty. Pencil skirts weren't designed for stepping up onto high chairs, but she managed, albeit in a slightly unladylike fashion. She looked around while she waited on the currently non-existent bartender. There were a few people sitting at the back of the bar, but it was relatively dark. They seemed to be having a quiet conversation and paid her no attention.

"Help you?" came a question from across the bar.

"Give me a shot of anything."

Tiffany had decided a few shots would give her a quick kick and remove the hangover that was coming back, and then she would have a few of her favourite whiskeys and get herself home. She didn't want it to turn into a late one, but shots were quick and then she would sip her whiskey for a nice glow. Getting home and slipping into her warm bed to watch a movie would be much nicer if she was a little tipsy compared to lying there hungover.

"Bizarro?"

"Excuse me!"

"The shot. Would you like a Bizarro?"

"Uh, yeah. I'll give it a go."

She slipped a ten-pound note across the bar and the bar man returned, gave her the drink and lifted the money. She knocked it back straight away. It tasted like sherbet dip but had a burn to it too. She could feel it reaching her stomach. Almost immediately she could feel a warmth rise through her and it felt as if she was tipsy already. She shook her head and rubbed her eyes.

"I definitely had too much to drink last night," she muttered to herself.

When Tiffany opened her eyes, the bar was no longer in front of her.

"What the fuck?"

"We will have none of that language here young lady," came a voice from behind her.

She spun around. She now faced an enormous chair next to a roaring fire where sat what could only be described as a black panther in a Santa suit. Even more strange was the fact that it was sitting upright in the chair like a human would. It genuinely looked like it was smiling at her.

"Did you just... Did you just talk?"

"Well, of course I did. Do you see anyone else here?"

"No, but, you're a panther."

"A what?" it responded.

"A panther."

"I am Santa Claus. Nothing more. Nothing less."

"Wait! Santa is a fat jolly old guy with a beard."

"Is he?"

It was definitely smiling.

"Yeh, he fucking is. What do you mean is he? Have you been living in a cave?"

"I've lived in many places, my child."

Tiffany could feel herself getting pissed off.

"What's going on? Where am I?"

"You are exactly where you are supposed to be, child," the panther replied.

"Will you stop calling me 'child'?"

Tiffany racked her brain for what could possibly be happening and wondered if the bartender slipped something into her drink. She shook her head, rubbed her eyes again and took a deep breath. Upon opening her eyes, she was still facing the black panther in the Santa suit.

"Okay. I'll play along. Why am I here?" Tiffany asked, trying to calm herself down.

"Only you can answer that question, child."

"I fucking told y…" Tiffany caught herself and took another deep breath. "Okay… How do I get out of here?"

"Well, why do you think you are here?"

After another few deep breaths and a mental lecture to not lose her cool, realising it wasn't getting her anywhere, Tiffany decided to try and talk it out. If it was anything like a bad dream or trip, the best she could do would be to try and keep it as happy as possible and avoid any bad outcomes.

"I'm guessing I have had one too many. Either that or I have been sucked into a low budget reimagining of Scrooge. Either way, I'm ready to go home to my bed, so if we could move it along, that would be just dandy."

"Tell me your thoughts on Christmas, my child," the irritating panther said. It had a low, smooth voice that Tiffany felt she could almost fall asleep to if she was in a better frame of mind.

"Well, I'm guessing it's to help me realise some life-changing affirmation, but I'm pretty happy with how my life is going, so, as I said, can we move things along?"

"If you are happy, you wouldn't be here. What are your Christmas plans, child?"

"My plan is to get home and wrap myself up in a nice warm bed. I'll spend all night watching cheesy Christmas movies if you will just get me out of here. Good enough for you?"

"Is it good enough for you?" came the response.

"Holy fuck, are you the Riddler or a fake Santa? Come on, how do I get home?"

"Just ask, child."

"Can I go home, fake Santa panther?"

The Santa panther smiled just as Tiffany blinked. As her eyes opened back up, she found herself sitting in a bar with an empty shot glass in front of her.

"No fucking way!" she exclaimed

Tiffany knew there was no way her drink

could have been spiked. Tripping rarely came and went as quickly. She checked her watch and only a minute had passed. She spun back around towards the bar, which had returned to its normal place and there was another shot in front of her. She knew she hadn't ordered another, but she wasn't ready to go home yet and the side of her that often got her into trouble told her to have it and see how the night played out. The other part was telling her to get straight home to bed where she would be safe, but she had never been great at taking advice from that side. She lifted the shot and quickly knocked it back. She got the same warm feeling, but this time kept her eyes open. Deciding she would keep an eye on the bar. Eventually, the need to blink was too strong. Her eye lids closed then opened and once again the bar was gone. She was less shocked this time. She spun in her chair expecting to see the Santa panther, but this time in front of her was her mum and dad's living room.

"What the actual fuck?" she said aloud.

The living room was exactly as she remembered it. Her mother and father sat in their arm chairs at either side of a roaring fire. They both wore a different pair of Christmas pyjamas. It was Tiffany's mother who had started the tradition of new Christmas pyjamas and socks every year. She would buy them all a pair. It was the only day of the year that her father wore pyjamas, but he did it gladly to keep her mother happy. Tiffany knew he was a big softy when it came to Christmas too.

"What do you think Tiffany is up to tonight?" her mother said.

"Oh, I'm sure she will be out partying with her friends. It's a shame when they get too old to come home," her father replied, looking into some far-off place.

"I really miss her, honey."

"Me too, dear, me too. She's an adult now, though. We need to let her live her life."

Tiffany could hear the sadness in both of their voices. She realised she was crying as tears ran down each cheek.

"Maybe when her life quietens down a little, she will come home and visit more," her mother said, sounding wishful.

"I hope so, I really do."

Tiffany wanted to run over and give them both the biggest hug and tell them that she was sorry, that she loved them and had no idea they missed her so much. She somehow knew that this time she wouldn't be able to talk to the apparition. It was like watching a video. She wasn't sure how she knew, but she knew she was right. More tears filled her eyes and she struggled to see. She brought both hands up to her eyes and rubbed them, trying to clear the tears away. As her eyes cleared, she was back in the bar and facing a plain black wall. She spun quickly round in her chair to the bar, and yet again, there was another shot.

Wasting no time, she slammed it back. She wanted to know if there was more to see. This time she closed her eyes straight away and began spinning round as she opened them.

Finish this one up with Tiffany going to the airport for a flight to her parents. Going to surprise them. Thinking about the warm cosy bed in her mum's house and thinking her mum will have new pyjamas for her, on the off chance she ever turned up.

This time, things were different. Tiffany was standing outside her parent's house. The strange thing was that her parents lived in the middle of a housing estate but the house in front of her stood on its own. It was unmistakably her parent's home, though. She could never forget the place she grew up. There was no time for contemplating why she was here or wondering if it was going to be one of those sad moments from the movies that made her reflect on everything. Her parent's house was under attack. There were green goblin-looking animals everywhere. They wore badly- fitting elf costumes. Most had humped backs with ridged spines that had torn through the material in some places. They ran around chaotically, going between standing upright and running on all fours. Some were throwing stones or bricks at the windows. Some of them were trying to beat the front door down and others were climbing up onto the roof.

Tiffany shook her head, trying to clear her thoughts. She looked down at the weight in her right hand to see she was holding a pump action shotgun. Strapped to her two thighs were two Dessert Eagle .50's— not that she knew what that was. Just that she had a gun strapped to either leg. She had never held a real gun in her life, nevertheless she felt like she knew how to use them. Her entire body was clad in black clothes, making her look like an assassin from a Hollywood movie.

When Tiffany began to walk towards the house she moved with purpose. Whether this was a dream, hallucination, or reality, she did not know. In any case, no green little monster was going to hurt her parents. She brought the shotgun up and pointed it at the first elf that noticed her and started running at her. She kept her calm and waited until it was close and pulled the trigger. The elf exploded into pieces and left a huge red blood- splatter pattern where it had been standing. Only its two legs remained. She pumped another shell into the shotgun and continued moving forward. By the time she got to the house, the shotgun was empty. She watched another elf run towards her, flipped the gun upside down and used it to deliver a home run swing at the elf's head. She absolutely obliterated the creature's head and dropped the empty shotgun where she stood. She had known she could have pulled a gun but something inside her wanted to smash the elf's head open.

Once again, she moved closer to the house. The creatures were everywhere. She drew the Desert Eagle .50 and started putting rounds into each of the mutated elves. She felt good as she did it. She watched them drop onto their front sides or back sides and squirm around. She knew they were suffering and that's what she wanted. None of them got a mercy shot to end their lives. They had picked the wrong house.

When all the elves in front of the house were dead, she started shooting the ones that had made it to the roof. She enjoyed watching them roll off and smash into the ground. Once she had cleared the roof, she walked around the perimeter. There were none at the back or sides of the house, but a few windows had been smashed in and she wasn't sure if any had got down the chimney. Knowing that the front door may be locked, she climbed in through one of the broken windows. No sooner had her feet touched the carpet than she heard a scream from upstairs. She knew it was her mother's voice.

"Not a fucking chance. Little green fucks," Tiffany growled, already moving through the house.

There were none downstairs. As she began to ascend the stairs, they started throwing things down at her. It did not slow her down. They retreated into her parents' room where she knew they would have found her mother. Tiffany kicked the door so hard it nearly came off the hinges. As she entered, she had both guns drawn. There were at least fifteen of the ugly little things in there. Five of them were holding her mother. She wondered if the things had murdered elfs and stolen their clothing or if this was what they looked like and this bunch had just gone bad. Either way, they were dead. She shot two in the chest and brought the guns round to shoot another two between the eyes. She looked back at her mother each time the triggers were pulled. She noticed that her mother kept looking into the corner. Risking a quick look, Tiffany saw two legs sticking out from the bottom of the bed. She knew instantly that they were her father's and that he was dead. Even though Tiffany wasn't sure if any of this was real, her eyes filled with tears. She didn't know when she got back to reality if her father would be dead or alive. She pointed the guns at two of the monsters that held her mother and just as she was squeezing the trigger, one of them stabbed her mother in the chest.

"Noooooo!" Tiffany screamed.

She began unloading her guns into anything in the room that was green. In a matter of seconds, nothing moved apart from her mother slumping to the floor. She ran over to her and put her hands behind her head. As she pulled her mother's head up to look at her, the light went from her eyes. Tiffany was just about to scream again when her eyesight disappeared. Everything went black and then she was back in the bar, arms resting on the bar, hands over her eyes and balling her eyes out.

"You okay little lady?" the barman asked from the other side of the bar, making his way over.

Tiffany was up and out of the bar in seconds. The street looked exactly as it had when she entered, but everything else had changed. She no longer wanted to go back to her apartment. New jammies and Christmas movies weren't going to cut it. She needed her mom. Before Tiffany knew what she was doing, she was in a cab and heading to the airport. She had no idea where the new bar had come from or what was in those shots she had. She had never experienced anything similar before and hoped she never would again, but on this one occasion she was glad she had gone in. She wanted to see her parents. She couldn't remember why she always put it off. She regretted all the time she had missed with them. Maybe she was just trying to prove her independence and had taken it too far. Maybe it was more than that, but she knew one thing. She would never miss a Christmas with her parents ever again.

A few hours later...

Tiffany sat on the plane waiting for take-off. She had never been as excited to go home. She had thought about calling her parents from the airport to tell them she was coming but had decided to make it a surprise. Her body buzzed with excitement. She knew her mom would have enough food in for an extra person, she knew they would be delighted to see her even though they would be sleeping when she arrived. She no longer had a key, so she would have to wake them up. She also knew her mom would have bought her a new pair of Christmas jammies, just in case she appeared. She really did have the best parents. She wondered if after Christmas it might be time to look for a new job, closer to home.

The End

Printed in Great
Britain
by Amazon